OLD COUNTRY SURPRISES

OLD COUNTRY SURPRISES

KEN SAIK

iUniverse, Inc.
Bloomington

Old Country Surprises

iUniverse books may be ordered through booksellers or by contacting:

iUniverse
1663 Liberty Drive
Bloomington, IN 47403
www.iuniverse.com
1-800-Authors (1-800-288-4677)

ISBN: 978-1-4759-4554-6 (sc)
ISBN: 978-1-4759-4556-0 (hc)
ISBN: 978-1-4759-4555-3 (ebk)

Printed in the United States of America

iUniverse rev. date: 08/28/2012

Grains of Sand Last

My grandfather died a little over a year ago. Since then, my brothers have pressured me to record the Ukraine research trip we shared five years ago.

"Mike, you're not retelling those stories to Grandfather anymore. Before you know it, you're going to start forgetting important details," warned Jacob, my insistent younger brother. "How do you expect your sons to value the stories you told Grandfather if you can't even take the time to write them down?"

I hadn't considered why I had avoided writing some kind of memoir or even preparing a PowerPoint presentation of the trip. I think in the beginning I had hidden behind the time I took playing with my boys: Victor, age three, and Steven, two. The demands at work after Dad promoted me to manager of scheduling and maintenance two years ago provided another excuse. That was also when Grandfather's heart grew so weak that he became housebound. Gram convinced me to squeeze in as much visiting time as I could. I suppose during this last year I could have used the time I spent visiting Grandfather to record the events of the trip he sponsored, but I didn't do it.

Then, Uncle Jim's request to visit a couple of days ago forced my hand. I could no longer delay reviewing the research holiday.

Face your guilt, I told myself. *You failed to meet some of Grandfather's expectations as a result of the research trip.*

Other than taking Ukrainian courses soon after I returned from the trip, I had done little else to develop my understanding of our heritage. I had managed to repress any uncomfortable memories of the trip, especially those surrounding Natahsa, an attractive young lady I met in the Ukraine.

However, recording the highlights of the trip would demand recognizing and evaluating Natasha's effect on me. I can't deny that her expressive eyes and engaging smile held my attention. Later, I realized she'd be a valuable asset in helping me to carry out the dreams with which Grandfather entrusted me. Natasha's imposing personality had clouded my commitment to work with her to dig into my family's history. For a time I succeeded in dismissing her, but that diminished my drive to develop the family tree that she started for me.

I know my family's perception is that Grandfather's plan for a paid research holiday to the Ukraine started around Christmas Day six years ago, but I think it began just before Thanksgiving Day. Mom and Gram expected my brothers and me to come and help make perogies for the Thanksgiving meal as we always had before. But we didn't. I know I didn't think anything of it at the time.

Then, the following weekend, Grandfather invited himself for lunch with me. I told him I would be at work. He said he knew that, but he tempted me by promising to fry up some perogies in the common room at work and to bring some ham from the Thanksgiving meal. That guaranteed, I'd accept. He knew my weaknesses well, but I'd have accepted his request to spend time over lunch without the food bribe. He'd always been a source of encouragement for me.

Grandfather came early, around eleven thirty. By the time I completed my morning duties, the perogies were ready—onions and bacon pieces were fried, and the ham was zapped in the microwave. He even brought a small container with sour cream. He and I were the only ones there, which was lucky for me. Otherwise, I might have felt I had to share some of the meal.

"Like it?" he began.

In my enthusiasm I proclaimed, "Oh, yeah."

"I thought you would. We, Gram and I, love to give you and your brothers leftovers like this."

I stuffed my face, paying small attention to the fact that he had taken very little to eat.

"That's why we were disappointed when we had little left over after the Thanksgiving supper."

"Yeah, everything pretty well went didn't it?"

I downed some hot tea that he'd also prepared.

"And you know why that was, don't you?"

I looked up to see him studying me. Without bothering to think about the circumstances surrounding Thanksgiving, I shook my head.

He leaned forward like he was about to share a secret.

"Because *you* and your brothers didn't show up. Gram, your mom, and I made everything ourselves. We sacrificed quantity. We didn't have enough time."

The memory of the tasks I had scheduled that day came flooding back to me. As soon as I finished swallowing, I interrupted.

"But, Grandfather, I had so much work here—"

I halted midsentence, because Grandfather's hand shot up as if to say, "Stop!"

"Mike, I'm proud you take your work so seriously and that you work so hard. You're just like your dad."

He paused a moment, letting the compliment seep in.

"But you need to remember why you work."

His next pause caused me to reflect on the nature of the stories he often shared. What came to mind were accounts about what life was like in the old days. The old days weren't just what life was like before his family moved to Canada. It was what life was like for his father and the generations before him. All were poor farmers—peasants. They survived poverty, the government, the weather, and the hard work. He praised the church and his family for sticking together and helping each other.

"The management position granted to you by your father prevents you from claiming financial woes. Your position gives you the power to set schedules *and priorities.*"

He stressed those last two words, and looked at me to be sure that I nodded my understanding.

"You must communicate to the company's clients that when it comes to family events, especially for events like Thanksgiving Day preparations, family comes first."

I'd stopped devouring my lunch. Grandfather completely captured my attention. At the same time his words brought me back to a time when I was about ten years old, being instructed about some matter of importance. Grandfather had sized up my situation perfectly. I hadn't even considered rescheduling my business plans.

"You have a position of responsibility, of leadership. You need to model appropriate values, maybe for the firm's businessmen, or maybe for the employees, but definitely for your brothers."

That last reference caught me by surprise.

"Yes, your *brothers*. You see, I've already talked to them. They confessed that after you told them you weren't coming to help Gram and your mom, they, too, felt comfortable bailing out."

I remembered them talking to me about whether I was coming to help. Grandfather was still leaning forward, toward me, like he was sitting on the edge of his seat, intent on reeling in a big fish.

"I want you to understand something. My concern isn't about the fact that we prepared a lot less food than we usually do. Everyone still had enough for the meal. It's the time we missed being together and talking and sharing tidbits about our lives."

His hand reached out and gently rested on my shoulder.

"Gram and I love you, Mike. We love hearing how you talk about solving your challenges and your excitement over your successes."

I smiled. I think he understood that the lesson was well received. Grandfather leaned back in his chair. His portion of the lunch began to disappear.

I couldn't help remembering how Grandfather looked forward to visits from his brothers. With the table cleared after supper, they'd drink coffee and talk about the old days. My brothers and I sat around the table with our pop or punch, if Gram made it. They always included us in their conversations. Either they'd ask our opinion about a situation, or they would ask us to finish a story that we'd heard dozens of times before. Then it hit me: Grandfather's brothers had all died. We were all the family he could now look forward to for tale-telling.

My brothers and I were as dear to him as his brothers. Grandfather did it again. He challenged my behavior, while at the same time showing me we were a valued part of his life.

How could we not try to rise to his expectations?

I wondered if I did that with the guys in the shop.

As I surfaced from my contemplation, he raised his hand, pointing the index finger to me.

"I have a question for you."

He washed down his food with the balance of the tea in his cup.

"I'm thinking about your Christmas present, yours and your brother's. I want to ask you if your schedule is too busy to take time out for something fairly important."

After my little lesson on priorities, he had to expect I'd be flexible. I guessed he planned on purchasing tickets to go see the Shumka dancers—the Canadian-Ukrainian dance troupe that was touring Canada. I had heard on the radio that they had some performances scheduled in Calgary for early in the New Year. Since we missed their Edmonton performance, I felt certain our presents were tickets to the show. Grandfather always attempted to involve us in activities like that, which involved our Ukrainian heritage, even if it was just as spectators.

"I can make time."

"Good."

That was it. He offered no further information. I waited. When he began stacking the dishes to take to the sink, I decided to pose my own question.

"What about your Christmas present? When will you give us a hint about what you'd like? Do you even have a wish list?"

My brothers and I had talked at length about it, but we had come up with nothing. Grandfather had everything he could possibly want, as far as we were concerned.

Grandfather had already stood up with the dishes in his hand. He looked down at me, smiling confidently.

"I do."

He paused, holding me in suspense.

"And in time I'll tell you."

"But when? Are you sure we'll have time to get what you want?"

"Oh, absolutely. And I can tell you that you'll have no trouble with the request."

Grandfather read my disappointment.

"Trust me. When you hear what I want, you will understand why I asked you to wait. You'll just have to be patient. Do you think you can do it?"

I agreed. I had no choice. It was a hard request to honor. As Christmas Day drew near and no hint came, my brothers and I felt we had to do something. We each wrapped up a bottle of vodka. It was more than he'd drink in a year. He'd been drinking a lot less in the last few years. Mostly he restricted himself to times when a toast was proclaimed. Still, he'd enjoy serving it to his guests.

* * *

Christmas Day came, and all the presents were distributed except ours to Grandfather and his to us. My brothers and I agreed that when it came to one of our turns we'd all three present our presents pretending to be the three kings who came to see baby Jesus in the manger. We saw only three envelopes left under the tree—Grandfather's gifts to us we guessed—so we took the initiative and presented our gifts to Grandfather on bended knee.

He laughed.

"Vodka, I'll bet."

We didn't try to disguise the shape of our gifts. He probably even shook it when we weren't looking and figured out what was coming. While we still knelt at his feet, he signaled for Mom to bring his envelopes. Grandfather handed one to each of us and asked us to open them.

A white card inside the envelope from our family travel agent said we each had a prepaid round trip to Lviv, Ukraine.

Our "wows" highlighted our surprise.

Clipped behind the travel agent's card was a check for each of us for two hundred dollars. On the memo blank of the checks were the words "research purposes." Our questioning looks prompted Grandfather's response.

"You wanted to know what I wanted for Christmas. Now I will tell you. I want you to find my birthplace. Take pictures of the area. Maybe, through some of the stories my father told me, I'll be able recognize some places. Wouldn't that be something?"

For a few minutes, Grandfather seemed to be lost in the past. I expect he was recalling some stories of places he heard from his father.

"I want you to talk to the people who live in that area, in particular the older people. You know, those who might recall stories of life before World War One. Bring back some of the stories you hear. Your agreement to this project is the present you can give to me."

I'd speculated. *Grandfather misses the talks with his brothers about the stories they heard from their father. If we come back with new stories it would be like his brothers were sharing memories with him again.*

My youngest brother, John, who was eighteen, asked if Grandfather would be coming with us.

His negative reply prompted John's question, "Why not?"

Mom broke Grandfather's silence.

"Grandfather's health won't let him go."

Our shocked reaction resulted in Mom's assurance.

"It's nothing serious, but it would be wise for him not to travel out of the country."

"If I can explain."

Grandfather's voice was soft, quieter than I had ever heard him talk before. I strained to hear his revelation.

"Lately I've been tired, like I don't have the energy I had before."

He spoke slowly, as if considering every word he spoke.

"I feel like there are things I still need to do, but I can't do them any more."

He paused; I guessed he was searching for how he wanted to proceed. Jacob took a breath to ask a question, but Grandfather's hand rose quickly, stopping the question before it started.

"Whether my perception is right or not, you know from time to time I have indicated I feel I have failed to communicate the elements and values of our cultural past."

I nodded remembering the post-Thanksgiving talk we had. I glanced at my brothers. They also were nodding and looking at me. Sitting at Grandfather's feet reminded me of when we were little kids waiting for him to tell us another story with its moral.

"I think I need help in this endeavor. I can't think of anyone who can do it better than people from the old country. When you are there, you won't have your daily responsibilities to distract you. That way, my hope that you will develop a greater interest for our Ukrainian heritage will have a better chance of being successful. Will you do that for me, for my Christmas present?"

I shot a quick glance to Dad to confirm I could take the time off from work. He'd guessed my inquiry. He gave a slight nod. It occurred to me then that my questioning look was thoughtless. Of course Grandfather would have checked that out first. He was that kind of thorough person.

Our thanks and hugs answered Grandfather's question. I doubt we needed his financial gift. I like to think we would have accepted his request to go on this research mission if he had just asked us straight out. I suspect his admission of diminished energy level had another motive. He'd subtly slipped in the news that his health was failing.

I wondered if Grandfather experienced regrets about how his son, my father, turned out. I know he said he was proud of how well Dad had built up his trucking business. However, Dad never took an active part in organizing any Ukrainian related festivities. He didn't even speak the language. Could Grandfather have been worrying that his grandchildren would develop a similar narrow perspective?

Or was it possible Grandfather thought, *My grandsons see my stories as an old man's ramblings, only a source of entertainment*?

* * *

By September of the next, year our travelling contingent had doubled. The increase started in January. Jacob, John, and I worried about our ability to communicate in Ukrainian. Even though John had just completed a course in speaking Ukrainian in high school, he wasn't very confident he could handle a conversation well. He convinced us to invite his friend Eric, who was fluent in Ukrainian. Also, Eric often wrote to a pen pal in the Ukraine. If we promised to visit Eric's pen pal, we could entice Eric to come. It worked, too.

A month or so later, Eric's older sister, Stephanie, asked me if she could come. Before I could object to having a lone female along, she added Melissa also wanted to come with her. Stephanie's smile suggested she knew she'd caused a rethink.

Melissa and I had dated a few times. I liked her, but when she quit returning my phone calls, I suspected I'd done or said something to turn her off. When I asked her about why she hadn't called back, she explained she'd been really busy. I concluded she decided I wasn't very important in her life, so I let it go.

I guessed the girls looked forward to an interesting holiday safe in the company of guys they knew. Since Stephanie and Melissa were good friends, it was understandable they'd want to go together. They had no particular sightseeing requests, so my brothers and I agreed they could join us.

Uncle Jim, my Mom's brother, surprised me when he told me that he and Aunt Susan planned to travel to the Ukraine in September, too. He intended to meet with Mr. Foresschuck, a friend of Uncle Jim's business partner. Uncle Jim and his partner hoped to invest with Foresschuck in the Ukraine. Mr. Foresschuck promised to show Uncle Jim and Aunt Susan around the area. I didn't think of it at the time, but now I wonder if my grandfather didn't persuade him to be in the area in case I needed some help.

My brothers, Eric, Stephanie, Melissa, and I flew Austrian Airlines on the second leg of our flight to Lviv—Toronto to Vienna. That torturous evening flight served good food on the plane, but my six-foot-two-inch frame struggled to find a comfortable position to sleep. The seats were so narrow and close together I could hardly move around. The following morning my neck was so stiff and sore I had to take a couple of Tylenol pills. I'd wished I had the money to sit in the business class section.

Midway through that second flight, Stephanie and Melissa surprised me. Melissa prompted a seating arrangement change with my two brothers. They switched to my row. Stephanie took the window, and Melissa sat next to me. Melissa didn't complain about being cramped. Then again, she is a good six inches shorter than I am. Melissa said she just wanted to come and talk. During this flight, she probed my interests, motivations, and hopes for the journey. Her interest and her support surprised me.

We landed in Lviv's new airport in the morning. Its construction had been completed in the spring in order to have it ready in time for the June 2012 Euro Cup soccer finals.

Lviv's Greeting

We cabbed it to the Eurohotel. Our rooms were very small. Jacob and I had less than a two-foot walking space between our beds and by the foot of the bed. The hotel's continental buffet breakfast was good, and the hotel supplied each of us with a bottle of water every day. I'd forgotten we were cautioned against drinking local water. The hotel staff provided us with a map of the city center area, helped us book two English-speaking city tours, and directed us to the nearest facility to exchange our American dollars for hryvnia, Ukrainian currency.

We received a little more than eight hundred hryvnia for one hundred American dollars. While the Canadian dollar was worth more than the US dollar in North America when we left, the Canadian dollar was about ten cents less than the US dollar in Ukraine. My first impression was that the Ukrainian financial institutions were a little out of step with the current market. Jacob reasoned that the Americans probably sell a lot more to Ukraine than does Canada, so their dollar is in higher demand, making it worth more.

That first afternoon, we walked around the immediate area, strolling along cobblestone streets, and noting packed, old trolley busses crawling down busy streets. Our destination was a huge pedestrian mall a few blocks away from the hotel. Together, using the shady side of the street, we strolled to the far end of the mall, stopping just past a huge water fountain. After reviewing the highlights of the walk, we realized we all found different attractions to which we wanted to return. We agreed to explore the shopping area in pairs and meet again in an hour and a half at the beginning of the street.

Jacob and I struck off together. Intent on snapping a picture of a fascinating piece of artwork, I led the way. Close to what used to be a curb along the street, I found an eight-foot tall tree made of metal black bars. Sculpted black metal birds and animals sat on many of the branches. While I admired this unusual creation and took pictures from different angles, Jacob consulted his tourist guide.

"They're gifts from the blacksmith's guild," advised Jacob, looking up from this pocket book. "Apparently there's an annual festival, and each year the blacksmiths provide a sample of their creative genius."

Before we reached our meeting point at the end of the mall, I took pictures of two more artistic expressions from the blacksmiths. One was a simple sundial, the other a giant stork's nest containing a miniature playground, complete with a slide, a swing, a teeter-totter, and a little horse, which might hold a four-year-old child.

A small group of tourists gazing at a wall mural of an old market square caught our attention. Instead of walking away after viewing the scene, the small group drew closer to the wall. Their fascination with the mosaic pieces stimulated our curiosity. After they left, Jacob and I decided to investigate. What they saw that motivated them to start taking several close-up and then distant pictures of the old town scene were four-inch tiles imprinted with the faces of people. Those tiles portrayed the historic site and demanded my camera record this unique work, too.

One side street generated an art gallery atmosphere. Mounted on and leaning against tables were oil paintings on canvas ranging in size from post cards to three-foot-by-two-foot creations. Some scenes featured religious figures, others rural locations or historical settings of cathedrals and forts. Woodcarvings and leather crafts adorned other tables. Embroidered work attracted many women to their kiosks. The exchange of calculators or pads of paper suggested prices were negotiable. While purchases took place, I could have spent the rest of the afternoon here enjoying the displayed art.

Jacob's interest centered on embroidered Ukrainian shirts. Buying one was on his list of things to do. He found one, a perfect fit. The 850—hryvnia price acted as a bit of dissuader. We both rationalized that purchasing on our first day in the Ukraine, whether a shirt or a painting, seemed premature. We had no way of knowing whether these were inflated prices for tourists. We also agreed that returning here later was a definite possibility.

As we left the small open market and approached the pedestrian mall, I noticed someone making a purchase I hadn't expected to see. An elderly lady, I guess in her seventies, received some money from a man in exchange for a small bundle of flowers. When we entered the open market, I'd seen the flowers and assumed they were decoration for the entrance to the area containing art displays. I'd also assumed that the one or two ladies sitting on the low, three-foot-long wooden benches were consumers tired of walking around. I noticed a small flower display on each of the four corners. Later I learned from Uncle Jim that those women were likely widows trying to live on their small pensions. Selling flowers supplemented their income.

Jacob and I returned to the agreed-upon meeting point early. Before sitting down on one of the benches used to block traffic from driving in the outdoor shopping center, Jacob pointed across the street.

"So much traffic! Drivers have to park on the sidewalks," he observed.

I looked down both sides of the street as far as I could see. He was right. It seemed sidewalks were as much for parking as walking on.

We stretched out on the bench. Before long, I wished the shadow of the two-story building to our right were longer. I thought of us as a couple of buns baking in an oven.

A drowsy feeling caused my mind to drift back to a particular painting I'd seen on the side street. Two simple, single-story structures, a house and a barn, each with golden straw thatched roofs, reminded me of Grandfather's request to learn about his distant (I assumed) farming past. Tall, red hollyhocks reached for the roof, while a partially worn path wormed its way to the front door. *Limited property use*, I concluded. I estimated the picture would fit in my luggage.

Was it the five minutes of staring at the painting, or me picking up and looking on the back for a price that brought the painter to my side with a five-hundred—hryvnia offer? Thinking I could divert his attention from trying to make a sale, I pointed to the name penned in the corner, and then I pointed to him. He nodded. He was the artist.

"*Dobreh. Duzhy dobreh.*" After voicing my compliment, I'd wondered if telling him in Ukrainian his work was very good was a mistake. I suspected it might initiate more of a conversation in Ukrainian than I could handle. Or it might encourage a bargaining process. I wasn't ready to buy. I was only curious about the cost.

"Four hundred hryvnia." He didn't hesitate in amending his original offer.

I'd immediately shaken my head. As I saw him take a breath, I guessed another quote was on its way. My hand shot up, just like Grandfather's when he wanted me to stop. It worked. I shook my head and turned away without another word being said. At the same time I wondered if he'd have accepted three hundred hryvnia. Had he made that offer, I might have accepted.

The sight of Melanie and Stephanie walking toward us about half a block away brought me back to the present. The two girls, dressed in slacks and short-sleeve tops, carried sweaters. A small plastic bag peeked out from beneath Melanie's sweater. I surveyed the rest of the street. John and Eric were nowhere to be seen.

"Couldn't stick to our agreement about buying nothing," I said, grinning and pointing to our two female travelling companions. I looked to Jacob for his reaction.

A broad smile graced Jacob's face, but he wasn't looking at Melanie and Stephanie.

"What you looking at?" I asked. I nudged him on his shoulder. It seemed like he needed a few seconds to replay the question.

"The girls," he paused. Then he added, "The women. Have you noticed? Almost all of them are wearing dresses or skirts."

I looked around. He was right. I saw only a couple of women in slacks like Melanie and Stephanie. *They might even be tourists too*, I hypothesized.

"Attractive, isn't it?" added Jacob.

I looked back at Jacob. "You sure its not just the young girls out there that's causing your face to beam like the sun?"

"Really. Don't you think so?"

"If you say so."

He tore his eyes away from three young girls walking away from us to look at me. I received a slug to my right arm for my disbelieving response.

Upon returning to the hotel, I checked at the desk for messages. There were four. As I expected, the message from the hotel staff confirmed the bookings of the Old Town (UNESCO World Heritage Site) tour for the next morning. The second message verified the walking tour of Lviv's original and restored buildings for the same afternoon.

Mrs. Balaniuk returned my call. She was the contact Mr. Foresschuck gave us through Uncle Jim. He suggested we contact her to arrange a tour of the Austrian-built Opera House. The clerk's scribbled note was short. "Tour of Opera House tomorrow at four o'clock. Confirm." Her phone number was at the bottom of the note. Even before talking with the rest of the group, I already considered asking the hotel clerk to move our afternoon tour to the next day if it conflicted with the Opera House visit.

Mr. Foresschuck also sent me a message. He apologized for letting business cause him to miss welcoming us at the airport. I hadn't even known he planned to be there. He said to make up for his slip up I should make a call to Mr. Kupchenko, a close friend of his and owner of a local brewery. I called. Mr. Kupchenko agreed to take us on a short tour of his establishment and provide a welcoming dinner, at which time we could enjoy all the beer we wanted.

That night at dinner we had some rescheduling to do. We all agreed that we had to try to squeeze everything in. The Old Town tour we kept as already arranged. I reported that before dinner I talked to the desk clerk. When he heard of our Opera House tour, he didn't hesitate to confirm our appointment. He also suggested seeing the National Museum and Art Gallery. He said they were very close to the Opera House. The desk clerk also said if we had any spare time, we could check out the souvenirs at the nearby outdoor market. Jacob really liked that idea. He wanted to price out other Ukrainian shirts. That revised schedule filled our first full day of touring in Lviv.

For the second day, we intended to take the walking tour of Lviv's original and restored buildings. The tour indicated it would finish in the afternoon, but it didn't say how late. We thought we might do some shopping to finish it off. During the morning of our third day, we planned go to the public library. I hoped, with help, I'd find someone who could give me a lead to Grandfather's birthplace. I know if we found it he'd be so pleased. That left us plenty of time to join Mr. Kupchenko for the brewery tour. I made a special note to contact Mr. Kupchenko the next morning to thank him for his offer and tell him we accepted. If he still really wanted to host the dinner, that would be bonus.

Our first walking city excursion was just as the desk clerk proclaimed it would be. It motivated taking many pictures and notes about points of special interest. We saw everything, from infected chestnut trees that were expected to disappear in a few years, to an extensive view from High Castle Park, to a Catholic church where we saw the largest wooden altar in Europe. We snapped pictures of several statues: one of the inventor of the first gas lamp, and one of the first printers of the Cyrillic script. A bridge built over a former weapons storage area caught our attention, too. Holes for guns in walls now located at foot level illustrated that roads had been built on the rubble of past cities. The guide also pointed out Hotel George, the city's oldest working hotel, and the hotel that once roomed former Russian Premier Brezhnev.

Viewing the Lviv National Museum, the Lviv Art Gallery, and the nearby open market soaked up the afternoon. Jacob found more shirts, but felt more convinced he wanted the shirt he saw the first afternoon we walked the mall. He liked the design better. The price was almost the same. At four o'clock, Mrs. Balaniuk, dressed in a navy dress and jacket, met us outside at the Opera House. Before starting, we thanked her for volunteering to give us a private tour.

She smiled and said, “It’s the least I can do for Mr. Foresschuck. He’s been a faithful supporter of the Opera House for some time.”

Her comment reminded me that I had to make a note to thank Mr. Foresschuck for this contact. Then I added thanking him for connecting us to Mr. Kupchenko. Before entering the Opera House, I asked to Jacob to remind me to thank Mr. Foresschuck for enriching our tour.

“It’s surprising he’d do such things for strangers,” I whispered.

After a moment Jacob responded. “Maybe not. He may be trying to impress Uncle Jim. He must really want Uncle Jim to invest in something.”

Jacob’s suggestion that we were being used started to bother me, but the fleeting impression disappeared after Mrs. Balaniuk unlocked the front door of the Opera House.

We entered what seemed like a wealthy aristocrat’s structure. A huge, white marble staircase greeted us. Partway up it split right and left, leading patrons to the second floor. A carved wooden railing bordered the staircase and the second and third floors. The sculpted, painted ceiling reminded me of some of the cathedrals we saw in the morning. Ornate, royal purple padded benches littered the sides of the rooms, inviting patrons to sit and soak in expensive works of art that hung on the walls. Ornate mirrors captured the presence of us commoners in a rich man’s entertainment center. I suspected tickets to attend performances here would be well out of reach for my budget. Stories associated with history and the works of art entertained us for half an hour.

At the end of the tour Mrs. Balaniuk said, “Mr. Foresschuck sends his apologies. He tried but could not arrange for you to hear any of the recitals. Everything is sold out.” As Jacob reached for his wallet to provide a tip for Mrs. Balaniuk, she waved it off. "No need. No need. Mr. Foresschuck has taken take of everything. Now come with me."

There's more! I thought we'd seen everything. Mrs. Balaniuk took us to Mr. Foresschuck's private balcony on the second floor. With a finger to her lips she indicated silence.

Then, in a whisper she said, "The orchestra is practicing. You may sit inside and listen for a few minutes. They shouldn't know you're here."

I asked, "How long?" I thought she indicated five minutes. Maybe she forgot about us, but we stayed rooted to our seats for a half hour before she came and escorted us out. We all agreed: the sound, the music—it was fantastic!

The next morning, after a late continental breakfast, the hotel shuttle dropped us off by the Opera House where we met the guide for our second city tour. By nine thirty we boarded the tour bus and were off to St. George's Cathedral. En route, the tour guide caught me signaling to Eric and John seated behind me. I pointed to box-like grey cement five—and six-story apartment structures outside our window. The custom-designed balconies on the drab buildings bespoke poverty hidden in Lviv. Some balconies stored bicycles, ladders, and weathered shelving. Others served as a place for laundry to dry. Some window designs enclosed their balconies, providing an interior extension to the living quarters.

"Stalin's structures," informed the tour guide. "Still standing. Better than Khrushchev's suites. His places were so small one barely had room to turn around in the bathrooms. Kitchens were barely four square meters."

The walking tour of Shevchenkivsky Park, the former seventy-hectare Austrian emperor's reserve, opened our eyes to life in the Ukrainian past. Single-floor wooden dwellings, most with tall thatched roofs, were common sites. We were told the straw thatched roofs needed replacing once every five years. A rich man's house with a shingled roof had distinctive carved posts on the porch. Symbolic representations decorated the door. The doorframe indicated people were at least six to ten inches shorter. The short beds confirmed my impression that people long ago were shorter than I am. The schoolhouse benches were long enough to seat three students. The width of their desktops matched that of their benches. In the center of the front wall hung a carving of Jesus on a cross.

Around one o'clock, the tour concluded with a Ukrainian dinner at Valentine Restaurant. This was a dinner, not a lunch. A cabbage based salad with cucumber and a generous sprinkling of diced tomatoes started the meal.

As our first course disappeared, a waiter slipped in behind the hungry patrons and filled a shot glass with a clear liquid. When the waiter finished, our guide introduced us to, and encouraged us to participate in a Ukrainian cheer of good will. He announced, "*Bud'mo.*" We were instructed to respond with a hearty "Hey!" He did that again, and we responded as directed, but this time with a little more confidence. Then, after the third *bud'mo*, we were to shout Hey three times. Then we downed the whiskey-like contents in the shot class.

A borscht soup appeared in bowls before us. Unlike Grandma, the restaurant served the soup with large chunks of potatoes. Platters of two different kinds of perogies appeared. One was made from a plain potato base, and the second contained a ground beef mix. Several bowls of sour cream awaited us, too. It was help yourself, and take as little or as much at you liked. Initially I took only a couple of each of the perogies. Second and third helpings followed quickly. Before the end of the meal, I devoured twice as many of the potato perogies.

Our guide rose again, to briefly describe the previous course but mainly to introduce the next one, holubtsi. These cabbage rolls were packed with a meat-and-rice mixture and a secret blend of spices known only to the restaurant owner's family. A bowl of thick mushroom gravy invited one to enjoy several helpings.

Then came what I suspected was the real reason for his announcement—another cheer. He raised his full shot glass and announced, "*Bud'mo.*" I glanced at my shot glass. It was full. I looked at John's and Jacob's glasses. They, too, were full. This round of cheers rose in strength and volume. We sat down and consumed the new serving. About the time we were digging into our second helpings, our shot glasses were refilled again, even if they were only partially empty. Melanie and Stephanie took only small sips, preferring to drink water with their meal.

When the tour guide rose again, I automatically reached for my shot glass like a trained dog. He extolled the apple pudding dessert as though he had created it.

"Generous quantities or sugar and cinnamon will leave you wanting seconds. Coffee or tea to follow. Board the bus in three quarters of an hour."

Then came the call for the cheer and our enthusiastic response.

"Just like you've been doing all your life!" shouted the guide with a laugh.

Tips given to the guide were usually fifty hryvnia. Everyone enjoyed the tour or the dinner and the non-stop treats in the shot glass.

Seeing the old dwellings at Shevchenkivsky Park reminded me of my promise to Grandfather. While I knew he'd enjoy the pictures we took, I also knew he expected us to search for his birthplace and talk to old people in the area about their lives. I decided we should go to the library to do a little research. The tour bus driver graciously dropped us off at the library.

I'd hoped I could find some resource person in the library who could find the location of Grandfather's birthplace. Their computer searches came up with nothing. The librarian worked with a number of different staff members. Still nothing. The librarian explained he couldn't help us because he said we either had an incorrect spelling or the place was too small to appear in their historical records. We ventured a long shot. The librarian promised to try to search government historical records, but I'd have to come back the next day. The staff member who had the access code had left for the day. He also recommended we talk to an elderly gentleman who worked weekends in the library. He had a very good memory for local details of the past. Jacob and I felt the two staff members gave it their best effort. We left, feeling our prospects for success didn't look good. We wouldn't be able to find Grandfather's birthplace.

We went to the Nobilis Hotel, where Uncle Jim and Aunt Susan had booked a room. We planned on sharing our disappointing news. As it turned out, we arrived too early. Uncle Jim and Aunt Susan were due to land that night. The clerk at the desk asked if we wanted to stay at the Nobilis Hotel. He apologized, saying he could only offer us deluxe suites, which was all he had left. I must have frowned after he informed us of the cost—we estimated over two hundred Canadian dollars a night. The clerk didn't pursue that effort again.

I recall showing him the birthplace my grandfather had written down, and asking him if he knew anyone who could help us find the location. I told him we knew only that it was somewhere in western Ukraine. I explained the tourist information center sent us to the library, and it appeared that the librarian couldn't help us either.

While our research up to this point disappointed us, it came as no surprise. Our Internet search drew blanks, too. Even Eric's pen pal reported to Eric that he couldn't help us. I was still resolved to continue asking around for information.

The hotel clerk looked at the name on the notepad but showed no sign of recognition. "I think I know of someone who might be able to help you," he said after a moment's thought. "Her name is Natasha. She manages a small inn in Chernivtsi, about one day's drive from here. She takes a great deal of pride in knowing the history around this area. If Natasha can't help you, she may be able to put you in touch with someone who can."

That was the best news I'd received all day. My hopes were raised even more when I found out that we could reach her inn by train. He smiled when he said their rooms were considerably less expensive, too.

For a moment I considered leaving right away. Then I remembered we'd accepted Mr. Kupchenko's dinner invitation for the next day. I didn't want to be rude. I suspected he would have accepted it if we told him we didn't have time for him to give us a tour. Missing the dinner, especially if he already made arrangements for the meal, wouldn't go over well.

I asked the desk clerk if he'd phone to see whether Natasha would be available two days later. I indicated we would be interested in rooms for the six of us. I hoped that would give the desk clerk an incentive to phone. It did. Rooms were reserved, and she would be waiting for us when we arrived. He wrote the name of the hotel and directions for finding it.

After we walked out of the Nobilis Hotel, Eric volunteered to find out what train we'd have to catch, and when and how much it would cost. When he was in the library earlier, he'd already been looking at trains to take us from Lviv to Kiev to visit his pen pal. He said it would be no trouble. He promised to do it next morning, when I returned to see if historical government records mention the place that Grandfather had written down.

I gratefully accepted his offer. I also wondered if his offer was meant to be a gentle reminder of the promise we made to go with him to visit his pen pal.

"And we can go on the internet to check out the tourist attractions in Chernivtsi," added John.

As we walked along the street, looking for a place to eat supper, my spirits soared. Perhaps hearing of someone who might find Grandfather's birthplace gave me the lift. I think I'd been feeling a little guilty for having such a good time in the Ukraine at Grandfather's expense. I didn't want to return home without accomplishing his objectives. I remembered disappointing him when I didn't show up to help prepare the Thanksgiving meal. I didn't want to disappoint him again.

The excitement about the prospect of success infused fresh energy into me. The momentum drove me through the evening and into the next morning. Even when the librarian confessed he couldn't find Grandfather's place of birth in the historical government records, I still felt confident that Natasha would provide the miracle I needed. John cautioned me that I might be putting too much hope in someone I hadn't even met. I dismissed his warning when Eric presented all the information we needed to take a train to Chernivtsi.

Before leaving the library, I phoned Uncle Jim to report our progress. He had no trouble recognizing my excitement. Unlike John, he offered no cautionary note. Instead, he invited us to share a celebration supper with him when we completed our research.

John, Eric, and I caught a cab to Mr. Kupchenko's brewery. While we arrived five minutes early, Jacob and the girls were late. They'd returned to the pedestrian mall, which we visited the first afternoon we arrived. Jacob wanted the shirt he'd seen, but he also wanted the girls' evaluation of the quality of the material and the workmanship. The plastic bag he carried confirmed Melissa and Stephanie approved his choice. That meant I, too, had a shirt. The girls also made some purchases. Before we could finish updating each other, Mr. Kupchenko interrupted our storytelling to introduce his assistant, who conducted the tour.

We began by descending into a basement museum. The assistant announced we'd find few other tours as enjoyable. Prompted by the many displays of machines and bottle designs, the assistant launched us into story after story about production changes or sales of their brew. I suspect at least a few of the stories were embellished for our amusement. Several small plastic glasses of different beers entertained our taste buds. He squeezed the one-hour tour into forty minutes, claiming that if he brought us to the boardroom late for dinner, Mr. Kupchenko wouldn't let him join us.

Once again we were graced by a four-course meal, starting with a cabbage-based salad. Borscht followed, with large potato chunks, but different from what we had the day before. Next we had potato pancakes, pork chops, and mushroom gravy. For dessert we ate a fresh fruit salad. Mr. Kupchenko also invited the managers from production, promotion, sales, and public relations. The latter had served as our tour guide. Several jugs of beer on the table meant we didn't leave thirsty.

The questions How do you like the Ukraine so far? and Is there anything in particular you hope to see? facilitated most of the table conversation. The latter question in particular opened the door for me to share the good news we picked up from the Nobilis clerk about finding a possible contact in Chernivtsi to help us find our grandfather's birthplace. When Mr. Kupchenko heard about our plan to take a train to Chernivtsi, he offered us an alternative.

"Pawelo. Doesn't your brother live in Chernivtsi?" asked Mr. Kupchenko.

"He does, sir."

"And don't we have contract renewals coming up with Mishel and the Black Castle Hotels in Ivano-Frankivsk?"

"Yes sir."

I learned later that Ivano-Frankivsk was on the way to Chernivtsi.

"Any reason why you can't do a little driving tomorrow?"

"Just have to make appointments. I'll get on that right after dinner."

"You still have a few days holidays from last year?" Pawelo nodded. "I suggest you take some starting tomorrow. Visit your brother's family for a few days. That should increase the window for making appointments with our hotels in Chernivtsi."

"I take it you'd like me to take the company van so I can give our guests a ride." Pawelo smiled, anticipating his boss's wish.

I started to object. While I saw Pawelo shake his head and try to explain how it was no trouble, Mr. Kupchenko interrupted him.

"This is no trouble. In fact you're doing me a favor. Mr. Foresschuck said I was to take good care of you. Doing this means he'll owe me. It is not often I'm in a position to have Mr. Foresschuck owe me for a favor." Mr. Kupchenko looked very pleased with himself.

"But what about Pawelo?"

"Oh, don't worry about him. He knows he'll being using the company van and company credit card for gas to see his family."

Mr. Kupchenko looked to his smiling employee. "Right?"

With a grin, Pawelo nodded his agreement.

"See?" asked our host, looking back at me.

"And while Pawelo is dealing with the contract renewals, you will be able to visit the historical Hutsul and the Pysanka museums in Ivano-Frankivsk. Then you can head on to Chernivtsi.

What else could I do? I shrugged my shoulders and accepted the arrangement.

"Good," responded Mr. Kupchenko.

He downed the rest of the beer in his glass. "I'll leave you guys to make the final arrangements. I've got something else I have to attend to now."

He waved good-bye as he left the room.

Driving to Chernivtsi Via Ivano-Frankivsk

Around midmorning the next day, Pawelo picked us up. Already it felt like the afternoon sun had settled in. As we entered the air-conditioned van, I thanked Pawelo again. He responded by thanking us, saying if he'd used his vehicle, he wouldn't have had the pleasure of a cool interior.

As we drove out of the city, we passed down a street lined with businesses sporting the blue and yellow Ukrainian flag. I assumed the many flags expressed nationalist spirit for the 2012 Euro Cup. Pawelo's disapproving grunt puzzled me. When he offered no explanation I asked what was wrong.

He waited for a while, and then he pointed at some other businesses on his left that also had flags hanging from their rooftops.

"See the difference?"

I shook my head.

"Sky blue," he said. "That's our color. Not like those."

He pointed to some businesses that had flags with a deep blue color.

"Imitations. Speaks of shallow Ukrainians." After a moment he added, "Like many in Kiev."

I sensed a note of animosity in his last phrase. I wondered what actions led him to such a conclusion, but I declined the temptation to ask him about it. Many stories from the tour guides reported on the oppression of past Austrian and Polish conquerors, but I detected no negative overtones to what they said. I guessed that time had diluted the pain.

I asked one of the guides what motivates Ukrainians to be an independent people. I expected him to say something about their religion, their dance, their art, or their language.

He suggested it was the desire to be free of foreign control that drove the Ukrainians to push for their own state. His unexpected answer left us quietly considering his response.

Pawelo ended the van's silence by beginning a little quiz about the Ukraine. I wondered if he felt uncomfortable with silence that followed his last statement.

"Anyone know what Ukraine's national flower is?"

John answered. "The sunflower."

"How about what our national berry is?"

Eric answered quickly as if he were participating in a contest. "Cranberry."

"What about our national bird?"

John's answer rang out just ahead of Eric's. "Stork."

"Let's try something harder," challenged our driver. "What two sounds in the English language are absent in the Ukrainian language?"

Whispered consultations took place in the back. For a little while it seemed as if the guests were stumped. Then Rebecca's voice announced, the "w" and the "th." Laughter filled the van when Pawelo announced that Rebecca gave the right answer.

By this time we were driving on what Pawelo called secondary highways. I couldn't help noticing that our driver kept to a speed at least twenty kilometers below the speed limit. I suspect the many potholes in the road caused the slow speed and the frequent adventures into the lane of oncoming traffic. A couple of times I expected the driver from the opposite direction to blow his horn. It didn't happen.

I commented. "Sometimes in Edmonton we have pothole-filled roads."

Before Pawelo could respond, John added, "But just in the spring."

"Are all your roads outside of the city like this?" I asked.

"The closer you get to Kiev the more you'll see double-lane divided highways, all of which are paved. It seems most government spending is reserved for the benefit of Eastern Ukraine."

As we passed through villages and towns, I saw many old ladies busy tending their gardens. The gardens occupied the whole yard. I wanted to snap some pictures, but remembered that women do not like to have their pictures taken. I doubted the gardeners would know or object if I took their pictures, but I wasn't certain how Pawelo would react. At last I saw a family out in a field by the road. I snapped their picture.

"They grow potatoes, cabbages, beets, whatever, and then at harvest time sell them to a fellow who brings them to the market for the urban population," volunteered Pawelo. "That way the grandparents make some money, the driver makes some money, and the people in the city have fresh food."

"Extra spending money," I said. "Nice." I remembered a long time ago helping my grandmother in the garden. Gram would give me a little extra money. That's probably part of why I developed a strong work ethic.

"A little extra money for the grandparents to take care of their grandchildren," added Pawelo.

"Take care of their grandchildren?" I asked, looking at him.

He pointed to another family weeding to prove his point. A closer look revealed an old lady accompanied by three preteen children.

"We don't have much work here. About six million people, mainly parents, have left the Ukraine to look for work in other countries. When they can, they send money back to help pay for caring for their children."

I felt uncomfortable. My money was to help me to buy candy for myself. I used picture taking to divert my attention.

Several times I saw a cow or two tied to a stake near the road, eating grass. Sometimes two or three ladies sat together, talking as they each watched their animals grazing. Family cow, probably needed for milk, I hypothesized.

Once, when we stopped for gas, I walked to the end of the parking lot to look at some people hoeing. A farmer riding an old wooden wagon came up the road. A single horse pulled the narrow wagon with sloped sides. I waved to him and pointed to the camera. He smiled and waved back. I took his picture. I'd seen several of those wagons while we drove in the van, but we always passed them before I could get a good shot.

I'd taken several pictures of partially constructed brick buildings. In many places several pallets sat idly near a structure. Weathered, boarded entrances implied no work had been done for a long time. I finally had to ask Pawelo, "What happened?"

When we were part of the Soviet Union, the government supplied people with the bricks and other supplies to build the house. When we became independent, it became the individual's responsibility to build his own house. Without access to mortgages, all construction stopped until individuals saved enough money. Many people haven't saved enough money yet.

While driving to Ivano-Frankivsk, I reflected on the matter-of-fact tone that I heard from the tour guides as they described the effect of their former foreign Ukrainian rulers. Pawelo's critical reference to Kiev hinted at a latent, unexpected anger. I decided to check my perceptions.

"Pawelo, you know I was really impressed with the factual accounts by the tour guides in Lviv. I was surprised to hear no hint of hostility," I paused for a moment, "for instance, toward the Poles, Germans, or Austrians."

"I would hope so," responded Pawelo. "If we want tourists from the rest of Europe to come here, we can't go around belittling them."

"So you're saying that there still is tension among Ukrainians toward people who used to rule over them?" I faced our driver so I could read his body language.

"Wouldn't you expect that? How would you feel about someone who always denied your identity? Told you there's no such thing as Ukrainian people? Told you you couldn't speak your own language?" Pawelo's voice grew louder. He must have detected it, because he took a deep breath before he continued.

"In the city, there's a greater acceptance of different people." He looked at me. "That's not always the case in the country, especially among the elderly and those who are close to them." He looked at me. I thought he was trying to see if I was shocked. Then, in a lower voice, he continued slowly.

"At socials and family gatherings, old stories are often repeated."

I thought of Grandfather when his brothers were around. Not only did they repeat stories of the past; they also taught my brothers and me to tell the stories.

"Many times they're given as instruction for living," continued Pawelo.

I remember concluding from many of Grandfather's stories: "Work hard and you'll get ahead in life."

As if making a confession to a priest, he stated, "Some of those stories work to perpetuate distrust for some people."

I couldn't recall any of Grandfather's stories having that quality. Without thinking I asked, "For instance?"

He looked at me for a long time. I almost pointed to the road ahead. Our vehicle hit a pothole. That tore his attention from me.

Then he made a point of trying to impress me that he was really focusing on his driving, turning away from potholes early, crossing over to the left side of the road, and then working back quickly. At one point I concluded he didn't want to share a story. I accepted that. Then he began.

"There's a story I recall my dad telling often." His voice was so low that I had to strain to hear him.

At that point I felt Jacob's arms press against the back of my seat. He'd leaned forward to catch the story better. I'd forgotten about him. Looking around, I saw the others were dozing.

"Remember in the early thirties, when Stalin forced collective farms on the country?"

I nodded.

Jacob replied, "Yeah."

"Well, many Ukrainians starved in Eastern Ukraine, you know, the part controlled by Russia." He glanced at me and then at Jacob in the rear view mirror. I indicated I knew what he was talking about.

"Some people swam across the river that separated Eastern Ukraine from Western Ukraine. All they wanted to do was to get some food from relatives. When the Polish government found out, they sent the military to guard the banks of the river. Anyone they saw swimming across the river was shot." Pawelo looked at me catching my surprised reaction.

"Two of my dad's cousins died. They were about his age. Can you imagine how my dad felt? I have to tell you, when my dad told us this story he never said the Polish government shot his cousins. He said they murdered them; they murdered his cousins." Again Pawelo looked at me and then in the rearview mirror at Jacob.

"Now, I have to tell you that a couple of times I tried to explain to my dad that it wasn't the Polish people who killed his cousins. It was the Polish government, a government that the people had no say in. He'd say, 'Yes, yes.' But he still had little use for anyone who was a Pole. So how would you expect children growing up in a country and hearing stories like that to feel about the Polish people?"

I nodded, suggesting I understood why hurt feelings would persist. The truth is I could only guess how one might feel in those circumstances. I didn't even know anyone who was a victim of criminal activity or government bungling in Alberta. We rode all the rest of the way to Ivano-Frankivsk without another word being spoken.

As Mr. Kupchenko suggested, we saw the historical Hutsul and Pysanka Museums, while Pawelo dealt with his contract renewals. We took many pictures, particularly of the Easter eggs in the Pysanka Museum, the place of the largest pysanka in the world. The museum even displayed a picture of Vegreville's pysanka.

When Pawelo picked us up, it was like a new day. The tension that silenced the passengers had disappeared. After dropping us off at the inn in Chernivtsi, as recommended by the desk clerk at the Nobilis Hotel, Pawelo gave us his cell phone number and promised to give us a ride if we needed one.

"Just call me," he said.

I think he was serious.

When I walked into the inn, I immediately knew this place was more suited to us—no business suits, designer clothing, or concierge.

This was a place for ordinary people, a place where our jean-clad group would easily fit in.

Before I could ask for the manager, a young lady with long, red hair welcomed us. Another lady shadowed her, a little older with black hair curled in just below her ears. As Mel and I neared the counter, I noticed the red-haired lady's badge identified her as Sophia, a trainee. The other lady was called Natasha.

Perfect, I thought. *Just the person I'm looking for. Things are finally coming together.*

When I told Natasha I had come from Canada, and I was researching my grandfather's birthplace, she broke into such a bright smile. From that smile I couldn't help feeling she couldn't be prouder. She faced someone who valued his heritage so much that he would come all the way over from North America to become more immersed in it. I told her that I was in need of some help, and without a moment's hesitation, she offered her assistance, stating that she recalled the phone call from the Nobilis Hotel a couple of days ago.

First, she registered us.

"Three rooms with two single beds in each?"

We agreed. Natasha started the record work. After copying my name from my passport she said, "And—?"

She looked past Mel at my brothers.

Her hint of makeup, light eye shadow, fingernail polish, and small, ruby pierced earrings, complemented her looks instead of becoming distractions. I tried to estimate Natasha's age. If I'd seen her anywhere else, I would've sworn she was close to my age, about twenty-five, but her position meant she had to be several years older.

Her voice broke into my contemplation.

"We run a respectable establishment."

Mel quickly jumped in.

"Oh, no! I'm with Stephanie."

She pointed to the other girl in our group. Laughter broke out behind me. I momentarily turned red hot. I realized that Natasha suspected I was waiting for her to put Mel's name on as my roommate.

Jacob stepped up with his passport and announced, "I'm the only one here who can stand his snoring."

After Natasha's brief chuckle, she asked Sophia to register the other two groups while she finished registering Jacob and me. Natasha assigned us our room and gave us our keys. She told me to come and see her in the office when I was settled.

I hadn't taken more than a step away from the counter when I remembered my medication.

Returning to the counter, I asked, "Could I have a small fridge in my room?"

"A bar fridge?"

"Yes."

"I'm sorry. No fridge. Hotel rules. We are trying to discourage drinking in the rooms."

That really worried me. I explained I needed the fridge to store my medication. She agreed to have one brought up from storage, although she cautioned me that it would take a little time to become cool. I must have had a concerned look on my face because she added, "Don't worry. There's no extra charge."

After unpacking, I returned carrying a small, plastic shopping bag. Sophia led me to Natasha's office. The moment I arrived, Natasha put away whatever she was working on, as though she couldn't wait to help me. The instant I looked at her, I sensed something different, more informal. Her navy blazer hung on the back of the chair. I didn't feel like I was addressing the manager of the hotel anymore. From behind a large, dark wooden desk she pointed to a red padded chair. Sitting in it placed me directly in front of her.

Again I caught myself seeing her as an attractive woman. A red ribbon now tied her hair back into a ponytail, highlighting the freedom of her movements. Her white blouse had the top two buttons undone. The desk clerks were buttoned to the top. Like the other clerks, she wore a bright red tie. Her tie dropped inside the top of her blouse and then poked out between the third and fourth buttons. The rest of the staff tucked their ties in between the third and fourth buttons. It was probably not the case, but I couldn't help hypothesizing: it was a sign that the boss could break the rules and dress a little differently. I liked that daringness to be different.

I told her my grandfather wanted me to know about the lives of the ordinary people, about things one would not likely find in history books, such as coping strategies, and how they'd hide portions of their crops in different fields so they'd pay lower taxes, or money would be stored in clay vessels buried in a manure pile.

Grandfather had said, "You'll only find those things out by talking to ordinary people."

Natasha's smile and nods suggested my grandfather's stories sounded familiar. Her reaction came in a few sentences in Ukrainian. For me, she spoke too fast. I picked up only a few words. I suspected she was testing me.

I told her I spoke no Ukrainian and understood only a little. Not wanting to appear ill-prepared for this project, I quickly added that my youngest brother, John, had just completed a course in speaking Ukrainian in high school, and Eric, his friend, was fluent in the language.

Then came Natasha's invitation.

"I guess you're as well prepared as you can be. Why don't you join us at our traditional weekend celebrations tomorrow evening? Usually various members of the community bring a dish for the supper, but since most households are still functioning in harvest mode, they won't have time to prepare anything. For the price of a drink they all can join in the festivities. The cooks in my inn prepare all the food. That'll mean a larger crowd than normal. You'll be able to meet a variety of local residents. There will also be singing and dancing."

"And lots of vodka, I'll bet," I added.

Grandfather had talked to me about the drinking parties. They sounded like an absolutely great time. That question brought one of the most beautiful laughs out of Natasha. *Typical young guy*, she probably thought.

"Yes, but the crowd is more of a family nature now, unlike the male-only patrons of the past. And you won't be staying until all hours of the morning."

"Will you be there?"

I figured if she would be there, that would be a bonus, an opportunity to get to know her even better.

"No, I will have left to visit my family in Lviv for the weekend. But don't worry. When you go to the evening celebration, you will be able to make several contacts. You might even begin to hear some interesting stories, too."

I told her I was interested, and the others would probably be up for a party too. She said she'd ask Sophia to give us the group rate if all six of us were going. Group rates were usually reserved for ten or more. Natasha even promised to talk to the master of ceremonies, a personal friend. He'd introduce us to the crowd. People would want to talk to us. Many of them would see it as a chance to practice their English.

I noted she scribbled some notes for herself. I was curious what Natasha meant by "contacts."

She explained. "Meeting people at the celebration will open the door to a further question-and-answer session from some of the older ladies, probably the next morning at the coffee shop, the one that's two blocks west of here. Retelling stories of the past is what these people love best. You and your friends would be a new audience, a treat."

Setting the bag on her desk, I gave her the note I received from Grandfather.

"Can you help me find this place?"

I told her about our dismal results with the Lviv librarian. Natasha took the paper and woke her sleeping computer. I watched her click away at the keys. After a time, a frown appeared.

Natasha had me write down my grandfather's full name, Thomas John Bennek, and my grandmother's full maiden name. She refocused on her computer. Her eyes narrowed, and her head leaned forward. Her concentration shut out my presence as she worked through possibility after possibility. I was already planning how I would tell Grandfather that I interviewed many elderly people in the Ukraine but failed to find his birthplace.

The clicking stopped, and I looked up into a winner's grinning face. She sat straight up. Before she could say anything I was heading behind her desk.

"You've found something!"

With my hand resting on her desk I looked over her right shoulder at the screen but couldn't understand a thing. As you might expect, everything was in Ukrainian.

"Yes, but not from the initial information you gave me. I looked into local church records for births. I found a Thomas John, but the last name is different. It appears your father's parents shortened their name from Benneshuck to Bennek when they moved to Canada."

I was skeptical until Natasha named two of Grandfather's older brothers and three of his older sisters. I never knew about the name change. As a matter of fact, I wasn't certain Grandfather did either. He'd find that interesting.

Natasha promised she'd do more research to confirm her initial findings. Then she showed me the spelling I'd given her for Grandfather's place of birth. The spelling didn't match any place she knew, unless she understood the letters Grandfather wrote to be an English phonetic spelling for his birthplace. Then a match appeared.

I couldn't believe it.

"There was such a place?"

"It's about fifty minutes from here. But it's not a town."

She turned in her chair to face her computer, entered some data, hit enter. Then she turned back to look up at me.

"It's like what you might call a hamlet, except I wouldn't even call it that. One might call it a community hall."

I argued that in the past Grandfather talked like this was the site of a town that was an important center, but Natasha corrected me again.

The community center building that now bears the name your grandfather gave was at first a very popular drinking establishment. If people wanted to describe where they were born, sometimes they made reference to some well-known local institution. For people in this area it was the name of a drinking establishment.

I was worrying how my proud grandfather would take such news. Natasha, probably reading my concern, updated me on the status of the building. Eventually it became the property of the church. Apparently there's a story there, but I missed getting it out of her. The church made it a seniors center that worked at collecting antiques and writing up the stories behind them. "They meet Sunday afternoons after worship and lunch," she said. "The elderly bring their antiques and their grandchildren to write up their stories. They conclude with a communal supper put on by the church members, mostly members of the seniors' families."

I could hardly believe it. I walked into Natasha's office with nothing except my ice pack. Next I was leaving with three places I could visit and collect stories of the past, exactly what Grandfather wanted. I even knew the location of my grandfather's birth. I had to convince the rest of the group to extend their stay another day there just so I could complete my research. I knew that wouldn't be a problem. Natasha told me they could accommodate us for an extra day. On a separate hotel notepad she wrote down all the addresses and contacts. Natasha even proposed to contact the priest in the parish where my grandfather was born and ask him to introduce me to the amateur museum workers, or as she called them, the memory-makers. I agreed, and she scribbled that action on her notepad.

I felt like there was nothing I couldn't do. Then a daring challenge stood up so close to me that I could reach out and touch it.

"What's wrapped in that plastic bag?"

Natasha pointed to the corner of her desk. She stood barely six inches away from me.

A risky move flashed through my mind. Time was too short to evaluate the wisdom of it. I either had to act on it then, or lose my opportunity. I bent down and forward a little, checking to the right and to the left as if I suspected someone might be eavesdropping on our conversation.

Then, with my cheek almost touching Natasha's cheek I whispered in her ear. "An ice pack."

I knew my actions and what I had said were incongruous and would require a further explanation, but it would give me another chance to drink in the faint perfume fragrance that Natasha wore. When she gave me her puzzled look, I moved in so close I could feel her hair tickling my forehead. I paused, enjoying the moment until I thought she was ready to pull away.

"I need a favor from you," I whispered.

Again, I waited a bit.

"I need you to store my ice pack in your freezer so when I leave in four days it'll keep my arthritis medicine at a cool temperature when we travel to Kiev, the home of Eric's pen pal."

Natasha's response was fast.

"So why such secrecy?"

The best part of her question was, without pulling away from me, she whispered her query in my ear. She was buying into my charade instead of interpreting me as an annoyance. I figured it was time to play my card.

"How do you expect a poor guy like me to admit I'm seriously flawed and that I need an injection to maintain my appearance of a strong, healthy, young guy, especially before such an attractive lady as yourself?"

Two hands on my chest and a gentle shove signaled my flirting had pushed things a little too far. Before I could be shot down I implemented plan B.

"Okay, okay," I began holding my hands up as if arrested.

I had just remembered telling her about my need for medicine when I registered.

"I thought the hotel has rules about doing special favors for clients. I mean you already extended a courtesy by supplying a bar fridge in my room for the medicine while we are here. And you emphasized that wasn't a common action for your hotel. Then I come along and ask for another favor. I just figured I'm pushing the limits. But I suspected if anyone could bend the rules, you could. I didn't want to broadcast this request and put you in an awkward position."

Believe me, I didn't have this line prepared when I began my move on her. It just came out in time.

"And if I could do that, why do you think I'd be willing to break any more rules for you?" she said.

She probably thought she had caught me as I spun my web of trickery.

"I thought you might be interested in how I'd express my appreciation," I began grinning.

I knew she knew I was setting her up for something, but she threw up no roadblocks. I could hardly keep my cool.

Slowly, I reached to my back jean pocket for my wallet. A simple bribe would be an insult. Besides I could never offer her enough money to do something she was unwilling to do in the first place. However, if I could intimate that the Euro bill I was extracting was a tool for something other than the obvious, I could have a little fun. Without looking up at her, I slipped my wallet back in the pocket and began rolling up the bill up into a tight roll. When I finished, I looked up at her. Still puzzled, she studied me closely.

"I see there's something wrong with your hair," I said.

I'd generated a what's-he-up-to-now? look. Her curiosity confirmed I could continue. As I reached up to the top of her head, I created a little opening in her hair before her red ribbon.

After I slipped in the rolled up bill, I confidently proclaimed, "There was something missing here."

My hand slid down the balance of her silky, soft ponytail, once, and then a second time. I could hardly believe she hadn't pushed me away yet. The third time I gently pulled down on the tail tilting her head up.

Those questioning eyes finally knew what my ultimate goal was when my lips met hers. Perhaps she was in shock at my bold move, but the expected slap on the face didn't arrive. I stretched my first quick-New-Years-eve kiss to more than twice as long as I had hoped for. Then I made my escape. Had I stretched the second kiss any longer, she might have thrown cold water on my second greatest achievement of the evening. As I headed for the door of her office like a thief who snatched a treasured jewel, I threw a quick grinning glance back. She was still standing there, just as I left her. I had to know if she was furious or flattered.

"When I've finished meeting with all these contacts, I'll let you know how things turned out," I said. I gave a casual friendly good-bye wave. If an energetic wave returned, all was well. If nothing happened, all the good work from earlier in the evening could be lost. I was turning to step out of the doorway when I saw a little acknowledging wave from her hand that still hung by her side. It was barely there, but I caught it. I closed her door and quickly left.

Aaahh, life is good.

The next morning I approached the front desk hoping to ask Sophia to extend our stay by one more day. In her place at the front desk I saw Erin, a young brunet who usually worked the evening shift. Natasha and Erin were busy with other hotel patrons. Natasha looked up, and I flashed a smile. Her index finger indicated she wanted to see me, but that I had to wait a second. No smile. Her business demeanor left me worried. Was I in for a tongue-lashing, or worse, a lack of support for my research? It seemed like she was going to extra lengths to satisfy the customer in front of her, just so I could stew in my own worries.

With his departure I stepped forward.

"About your report—" she started and then momentarily left me hanging.

I have no doubt she knew she had me tied in knots. Then, the corner of her mouth betrayed a hard-to-keep hidden smile.

"Do you think you could make your report Sunday evening at supper with me?"

Her smile broadened and tension left my face.

"Say seven thirty?"

"No problem," I answered as if I didn't have a care in the world. I knew my brothers would understand if I didn't eat supper with them. We'd talked about how good-looking Natasha was.

Then I caught the bus to the car-rental company that Sophia had called so I could rent a van. Eric, too, had a couple of places he wanted us to see. The night before we'd decided that we didn't want to impose on Pawelo any more than we had.

After I told them of Natasha's recommendations, John and Eric took over the planning for the next two days. The Fortress Khotyn, first built in the twelfth century, topped the list for Friday. This must-see site was credited for saving all of Europe from Turkish domination. Here, in September 1621, a Ukrainian Kozak army of forty thousand led by Hetman Sahaydachney defeated a three hundred thousand strong Turkish army. Eric also included Fort Kamienetz-Podilsky, a UNESCO World Heritage Site. Pawelo assured him we could see both in the same day. The weekend harvest celebrations for which Natasha gave us discounted tickets would follow.

After the anticipated coffee shop question-and-answer session, John wanted to explore the National University of Chernivtsi, another UNESCO World Heritage Site, built in 1864 and 1882. It had been the official residence of the Orthodox Church leaders of Bukovyna and Dalmatia. On the same day we could also see the Bukovyna Diaspora Museum. Pawelo said there was a room dedicated to the dispersion of Ukrainians in Canada. He was right. They even had a picture of William

Hawerlak, noting he had been a four-time mayor of Edmonton. On Sunday we slept in and did some of our laundry before preparing to meet the memory-makers in the afternoon.

* * *

The four days at Chernivtsi flew by faster than our first three days in Lviv. I felt that in Chernivtsi I really honored Grandfather's research mission. I had Natasha to thank for that, too. However, none of those accomplishments were on my mind, when I went to join her for the arranged supper. Erin, dressed in the hotel's uniform of a navy skirt and blazer, and white blouse with the red tie, escorted me to a private dining area, which Natasha had booked. I wondered, *Could I get off easy by just telling her that I succeeded in meeting Grandfather's hopes?*

We entered through a door labeled "Conference Room." A number of square tables neatly arranged in three rows greeted us. Only one table, bathed in a soft orange glow from wall lamps on either side of the table, invited dinner guests. Natasha stood before that table and a tall window looking out at the trees' fall display of color. Erin stopped in the middle of the room and waited for Natasha to turn around. The wait was short but clearly evident. I couldn't help thinking that this demonstration of authority was for my benefit. Natasha had something on her mind.

Turning around and glancing at her watch, Natasha greeted me with, "On time. Good." Before I could respond she asked, "You drink white wine?"

Instructions to Erin in Ukrainian followed my nod.

She watched as Erin left and then said, "I hope you don't mind. I took the liberty of arranging our meal in a more private atmosphere.

I thought considering what you would be reporting it might be more appropriate. Besides, we'll likely have no interruptions here."

I immediately became suspicious. She knew I must have heard some uncomplimentary stories about her aristocratic past. She knew that the men at the senior center probably had complained about relentless tax collectors. And she probably knew that the elderly ladies at the coffee shop grumbled about the booze parties thrown by the nobles to suck every last cent out of the peasants' end-of-the-week paychecks.

"Sounds good to me," I responded confidently.

"Besides, I thought you'd enjoy this view."

She stepped aside, putting herself in front of the navy curtains. Her right hand gestured to the trees outside that were dressed in their coats of green that melted into a sheer of limey yellow and splashes of gold.

My eyes were half a step behind the message of my ears. They couldn't help lingering on the vision of this pony-tailed lady with a larger red ribbon in her hair. Her white blouse with the top two buttons undone spotlighted the smooth red buttons the size of pin cherries. Wrapped twice around her neck and bordering either side of those buttons hung a white scarf with matching red splotches. Large ripe raspberries came to mind. Her matching navy pear-shaped skirt drifted gracefully, following her lead as she slid to the side.

I was glad I decided to leave my jeans in the room and wear the only pair of dress pants I brought. The olive green slacks and matching sleeveless sweater accompanied a light green shirt. I'd even buffed my black shoes at Eric's suggestion.

"Yes, it makes me feel right at home."

I shifted into gentleman mode and pulled a chair out for Natasha to be seated.

"It's a good feeling," she said.

"Then I take it you had a good weekend since you took time to visit your parents," I said, sitting opposite her.

"My father was entertaining some out-of-town guests so we didn't spend much time together. He doesn't often spend so much time with guests. They must have been very important."

As Natasha was talking, Erin appeared, poured the wine in our glasses, and left the bottle in a freestanding silver wine cooler. She left without a word.

"I took the liberty of ordering the food for us tonight. I hope you don't mind."

"Risky!"

"Perhaps. But I think you'll approve. You see, I'm a firm believer that knowledge is the path to a brighter, easier future."

I thought she'd expressed an interesting philosophical position, but I couldn't see its relevance to our situation. Before I could quiz her, the kitchen staff began bringing in the dishes for the evening. Borscht came first.

"*Smatchnoho*," announced Natasha as the bowls were placed on our table.

I recalled one of our tour guides using the Ukrainian invitation to eat up.

"*Dyakuyu*." I was surprised at how automatically I responded with the Ukrainian thank you.

I couldn't believe it. My first few spoonfuls confirmed the borscht was done just the way I like it: beet stems and leaves, a generous serving of shredded cabbage, with some diced carrots and some peas. Before I was even half finished, a large bowl of perogies appeared, with an ample supply of sour cream and fried onions. Then came ham, kubsa (a garlic sausage) and holubtsi (traditional Ukrainian cabbage rolls). I thought of Gram serving a meal at her place. It felt like I was celebrating a special occasion.

I couldn't help expressing my pleasure at the spread before me. Natasha's content smile made me wonder what hidden purpose this meal was serving. I thought of the elderly ladies' stories about the weekend drinking parties. *For what was I being set up?*

As I was finishing my soup, Natasha asked, "How'd your research go?" I told her that my brothers and I had found out many more stories than I had hoped for.

"At first, on Friday night and Saturday morning at the coffee shop with the elderly ladies, we struggled trying to understand each other. Eric was a big help in clarifying stories. But Ava—She was unbelievable! She helped a lot."

"Yes. Ava has a remarkable aptitude for language," commented Natasha. "I've heard as a child she picked up Russian and German quickly. For the longest time she and her family kept that a secret from the authorities."

I took Natasha's smile as an approval of Ava's ability to fool the government.

"Later, when tour groups came to see Ava's Easter egg displays, she learned English from one of the English Christian missionaries."

When I commented about Natasha's knowledge of Ava's personal history, she admitted she took seriously the responsibility to know the people in her community.

Sitting up, Natasha asked, "Did you enjoy the Friday evening celebration?"

"It was a very entertaining evening. A group of young dancers who were performing that evening joined us. Their English language was pretty good, too." We took turns introducing ourselves. After each turn a *bud'mo* cheer rang out, just like what happened on our second city tour in Lviv.

"And I'll bet your shot glass always had horilka," said Natasha with a smile.

I'm sure she remembered when I had asked earlier if plenty of vodka would be available. "You're right. But isn't it *horivka*? The dancers said real Ukrainians call their drink horivka." *Horilka* is Polish for "vodka."

"Oh yes, of course," replied Natasha smiling. "Anything else?"

"Yes. Our table guests introduced us to the *kolomeyka*. One by one, a person from a circle of dancers pulled us into their group. In the center we received a welcome hug from a couple of dancers. Then we joined the ring of dancers. After circling once or twice, they called out, 'Another Canadian.' Someone in the ring dropped out and brought another one of us to join them. When we were all part of the circle, some of the dancers went into the center and demonstrated some challenging steps. I'll tell you—I can't believe the energy they have! It's like they're preparing for Olympic competition."

After a few spoonfuls of the hot soup I continued. "Later, during the midevening break, we met the dancers outside the hall, where they encouraged us to try a few of the simpler dance steps. I laughed at a few of my brothers' clumsy moves, until I was dragged in. The dancers' encouragement extracted a promise from John to try to take some lessons at home. Eric said he'd join him." Natasha chuckled when I told her I guessed my clumsy efforts didn't warrant encouragement. She seemed pleased that we had a good time.

I told her that the priest's introduction to the memory-makers enabled us not only to hear their stories, but also to take pictures of several antiques and the stories that accompanied them. The little boys, their grandchildren, who were writing down their grandfather's stories, helped translate the stories they'd written down or just heard. I shared the story John told me he heard about the baptismal certificates.

"One of the elderly men showed John real and forged baptismal documents. He'd changed the date on one certificate so one of his sons could avoid military service longer. The noble's servant hadn't bothered to check with the priest, so the father got away with the ruse. John had taken a picture of the two documents."

I said, "I know my grandfather will love that story."

Then I told Natasha about buying a very special Easter egg from Ava and asked her if she would mind forwarding an envelope with some extra money for a purchase I made. Natasha agreed without hesitation.

She raised her wine glass and proposed a toast.

"To a successful research."

We clinked our glasses and sipped the wine. It was the best I recall ever drinking. I switched our conversation to the food that had been served and how it was just like what my parents and grandparents had made.

Natasha patiently sipped her third glass of wine. I worked on my third, but smallest serving of food.

"Anything else you learned?"

I took a long sip of my wine while I dealt with the uncomfortable feeling I was a child caught by my parents. They not only knew when I did something wrong, but also what it was. All they had to do was get me to admit to it. I partially dismissed that feeling by telling myself I knew I hadn't done anything wrong. Still, I also suspected Natasha knew I heard stories about aristocratic greed and manipulation. Neither the memory-makers nor the elderly ladies at the coffee shop complimented the nobility. Could I convey such a thing to a gracious host?

I confirmed I'd take home stories that would corroborate Grandfather's tales of hardship and poverty for peasants of Ukraine's past. I told her that around ten in the morning Eric and my brothers met eight ladies in the small coffee shop, which she had told us about. They sat crowded around two tables the size of card tables, pushed together. When we arrived, they pulled another table in and spread themselves around it, leaving room for us to sit among them.

After a little small talk in response to me sharing my grandfather's instructions to us, the ladies narrated story after story about their husbands putting in a full day of work, coming home, and then squeezing several hours on their own little plot or repairing their house or fence. At times the men didn't even finish eating their supper because they were so tired. And this happened six days a week all year round. The men frequently spent Sundays sleeping, recovering from their work. Respect for their husbands' tremendous efforts showed in the many stories of self-sacrifice.

"Hear anything unexpected?"

I concluded Natasha knew how bitterly the elderly ladies complained about the weekend drinking parties. She wanted it out in the open to deal with. She rightly assumed it tainted my impression of her and her ancestors.

I narrated my findings, hoping my own disgust didn't surface.

"Frustration over their husbands' heavy weekend drinking overshadowed the men's work efforts. Many times the elderly ladies at the coffee shop reported they never knew when or whether their husbands were coming home at night. In the winter the women were haunted by the fear their husbands would freeze to death if they drank too much and couldn't find their way home. They worried until their men finally stumbled into the house. With the shortage of food, some complained about the money *wasted* on alcohol. Other wives directed their anger at their inability to put an end to such *foolishness*."

Natasha nodded as I related these concerns. I felt annoyed. The information didn't seem new or disturbing to her. She sat as relaxed, sipping her wine, as she had been when I started telling her about the women's position.

I told Natasha I raised the wives' concerns with some of the men at the memory-makers gathering. Unanimously, the men, even at their present age, still valued their weekend drinking. They said it was the only time they dared voice hostile concerns about the government or those they worked for and hope to escape punishment. They believe their overconsumption or even appearing to be drunk protected them from whom they denounced.

Natasha's reaction to that segment of my report can best be summed up by this comment: "Interesting how different perspectives bring new understandings."

Then she fell into silence, expecting more stories. I thought about whether I should continue. I concluded she probably knew about their bitterness. I decided to be blunt and present the most damaging aspect of my research.

"The coffee shop ladies faulted the aristocracy for much of the peasants' poverty."

I didn't tell Natasha that the ladies pointed out Natasha's noble bloodlines.

"They blamed the aristocracy for promoting the weekly drunken bashes just so the aristocracy could sell liquor to their workers and thus take their money back and continue to imprison the peasants in a state of perpetual poverty or slavery. In the winter it was even worse. The nobles convinced some men they should stay at the inn instead of going home. That way more money could be drained from them."

The peasants never had a chance to buy their freedom. In reality it was an unattainable dream dangled before them.

"I imagine Ava was one of the ladies leading the discussion." Natasha still appeared unaffected by my revelation.

I thought her suspicion of Ava strange. Ava had nodded in agreement with what the other ladies said, but she never spoke a word. Actually, Ava's asking me to send the rest of her money by way of Natasha suggested a degree of trust. I began to think Natasha didn't know the people in her community as well as she thought.

I informed Natasha that so far Ava had only nodded in agreement. Her name came up only when I asked if I could be directed to someone who could show me some really good Easter eggs. I stated I had purchased some eggs at the Pysanka Museum, but I was after something special to take back for my grandfather, to kind of thank him for enabling us to take this research trip.

Ava's Easter Eggs

A couple of ladies told me I would be able to buy traditionally painted eggs at the church-owned community center, but for "special" eggs I needed to talk to Ava, a heavy-set lady with white hair combed straight back. From the sound of her voice and the wrinkles on her face and hands, I estimated she was around eighty or eighty-five years old, easily the oldest person there. Ava graciously invited us to her home later in the afternoon to see the work she did.

When the boys and I went, I was surprised to see that most of Ava's place was a workshop. Displayed throughout the house were tables with eggs in various stages of development. Tools and paints were neatly set up at the back on the tables. Dozens of shelves stored painted eggs. I made the mistake of comparing her place to a little factory. Like ignorant children, we were directed to a table for a history lecture.

First, she taught us about the pagan and Christian tales connected with the egg. A bowl of decorated eggs was often kept in the home in the belief that they would keep the family healthy. An egg with roosters would help the man conceive children. As long as the eggs continued to be decorated, the world would continue to exist. For some, spots on eggs represented tears from the Blessed Virgin Mary. The tears had fallen on the eggs that she carried to the soldiers near the cross of Jesus. Mary had come to beg the soldiers to be less cruel. Those dots represented suffering. After Easter Mass, Ukrainians exchanged decorated eggs as a sign of fondness and even forgiveness.

Part two of her lecture turned to the craft of decorating the eggs. She began with factors for the careful selection of the egg. Hearing the passion that she poured into describing the intricate design preparation, and the thought that went into selecting the symbols and the colors that adorned the egg, I realized the factory comparison might have been insulting. This process of painting the Easter egg was a loving, creative art effort.

As she concluded her talk about the meaning of various symbols and the colors depending upon their context, she explained that patterns and their meanings developed over time. Knowing the significant meaning of the creation on the egg meant a sharing of meanings between the creator and the one who received it.

"Let me show you."

She began plucking eggs from the shelf nests.

"Here, what does this one say to you?" Ava asked, handing me an egg. Each of the others in our group also received an egg.

I felt like I was in an art gallery, interpreting a canvas painting. About 85 percent of the center of the egg was a dull black, something your eyes wanted to pass over quickly. The small, star-shaped, white top had faint traces of a yellowish gold. The larger wide bottom was mainly orange with streaks of red shooting out. Smudges or smears of black begged for a cleaning cloth.

"Heaven and hell," I postulated and pointed to the top and bottom of the egg.

"Very good. Keep going."

On each of the four sides, narrow, red, Roman-like columns rose, dividing in the center of the egg into three stems, each ending with a fist. Resting on the fist scratched in thin purple lines was a large crown.

"The king," I suggested.

"Tsar or aristocracy," corrected Ava. "Why thin lines and not thick like this?"

She pointed to the egg that Jacob was studying. The purple lines of the crown on that egg were five times heavier. Jacob looked at my egg.

"Weak ruler?"

"In the mind." Ava nodded. "Notice where on your egg the crown sits."

It occupied a significant part of the top half. Again she showed me Jacob's egg with the thick crown outline. It was mostly below the halfway mark. I noticed the crown on Jacob's egg had green and red spots—jewels, I guessed.

"More government interference in the lives of people," I guessed, pointing to the crown on my egg.

"Aristocratic interference," Ava proclaimed disapprovingly.

Pointing at a wide, wiggly, red snake on the crown of the egg I held, I ventured, "Evil."

Its head and tail flew above the crown.

"Or source of harm."

The tear-like red dots beneath the crown I guessed showed suffering—suffering of the common people.

"Notice how organized the dots are."

"Deliberate suffering," I said.

"Torture," I concluded.

"Good," complimented Ava.

She smiled, as she sensed I was beginning to realize the horror her ancestors survived.

The background of the upper third of the egg faded to a smoky grey, like a heavy fog. On each of the four sides stood narrow, brownish-golden sheaves of wheat, waiting to be taken to the barn. Squeezed between the wheat was a heavy table in bold blue. That blue, Ava said, could symbolize good times, even paradise. On the table was a single round loaf of bread.

Sustenance, I assumed.

Painted under the table was the symbol of a few chickens, a rake and a shovel.

An egg really is like a small painting, I concluded.

I was about to proclaim, in spite of all the adverse conditions of her ancestors, that the peasants still managed to create a good life. Then I noticed the ends of the rakes' and shovels' handles were short and jagged. Beside them were matching jagged stick stubs.

Broken tools, I concluded. *Hard Life.*

A red arrow piercing one of the two chickens beneath the table confirmed my hypothesis.

A red streak shot out from a smoldering base of the egg, passing right by the crown: *a spear straight from hell.*

"Survival in such an atmosphere was a miracle," I said, after sharing my interpretations of the rest of the egg. "It reminds me so much of Grandfather's stories."

I began to understand why Grandfather's face just shone when he heard stories of our perseverance, whether it was in studies or sport. It must have been like a confirmation that we had his ancestors' genes. We'd keep trying. We'd never give up.

Ava stood up and lightly patted me on my shoulder twice.

"They aren't memories we can purge," admitted Ava sympathetically.

She turned and talked to each of my brothers and Eric, coaching understanding of the story portrayed in their eggs. As I listened to the tales emanating from each of the eggs, I realized they all told of a dark past. The unique stories spoke like voices of individual peasants; spirits of our ancestors Grandfather used to call them. Each egg was a work of art, an original work of art.

No wonder Grandfather was so proud of his family's past. Many of us had latent artistic talents.

I searched for some sign that would identify the creator of this work, but couldn't find any. In response to my question Ava pointed it out, barely noticeable under the king's crown scratched in light gray like a design going around the egg: A V A H. A V A H. A V A H. A V A H.

I couldn't help objecting.

"Why so small, so vague? It should be in white, or gold, or even that light blue. You create such wonderful art!"

"I am not worthy," Ava confessed. "I am full of hate for those who created our misery. The darkness that's within me seems to always pour out in my work. Forgiveness for most aristocrats hasn't been forthcoming. How can I take pride for that sin?"

As she collected her masterpieces from Eric, Jacob, and John, I clung to mine.

"Could you tell us how much this is worth?"

I was afraid of her answer. It would be very expensive, but I had to know if it was possible to purchase it. I knew Grandfather would fall in love with it. There could be no better souvenir to bring back than the egg and its story.

Ava stood still, contemplating, as if there were no set price. "You ask because it is something for yourself, not for some business purpose?"

"Yes."

I sat stuck to the wooden stool waiting for her response.

Ava noted the other boys nodded in agreement. Again she remained quiet, holding us in suspense.

"Fifty Euros."

"Each!" exclaimed John.

The surprise in John's voice matched what Ava saw in all four of our faces. We'd seen eggs in Lviv for one fifth of that price. I shot a "silence," command to them, hoping we'd find an opportunity to talk privately.

"Yes, but don't feel like you have to buy any of these eggs. The group that you visit tomorrow will have more traditional ones, which are much less expensive. I'm honored that you came and showed so much interested in my work and wanted to know more. I just hope that I've created some lasting memories for you. I paint these eggs as a way of soothing my soul, much like one who writes in a journal. I have no marketing plan, as some tourists before you have learned."

"Can we at least take pictures of the eggs that you showed us?" asked Jacob. He sounded like he expected a negative reply.

"Certainly!"

Ava returned the eggs, and we all snapped our pictures, grouping the eggs together and taking close-ups of our individual egg and each of us studying our egg.

"If you're not in a hurry, I think I have another egg or two you might be interested in. They are very special. There's one in particular, Mike, that I think your grandfather would like to see."

Ava was looking directly at me.

"Would you like me to see if I can find them?"

I agreed, welcoming the opportunity to have a private conversation with my brothers. As she left, I signaled the boys to huddle together. In a low voice I announced I was considering buying the egg that Ava and I had talked about.

"Are you crazy?"

I expected that reaction from Jacob, my money-conscious brother. Had I seen these eggs in a shop without the stories from Ava I would have had the same reaction.

"No. Seriously. I want the egg she told me about. I want it for myself. It reminds me of Grandfather's stories. When I share that with him he'll just love it too. I think it's the kind of thing he'd want us to spend our research money on. Just spending research money to cover the cost of traveling to dig up information is kind of a rip-off. But bringing something like this—" I held up the egg, "is what would put a smile on his face."

"I don't know. It still seems very expensive."

Jacob's objection lacked the conviction of his first reaction.

"Jacob, think of it this way. It's an investment. You're buying an original piece of artwork. Who knows what it could be worth in the future! This is a one of a kind. Who do we know back home that would put so much time and effort into work like this?"

John was the first to join me.

"I think Mike's right. Grandfather would be happy to see us buy these eggs. I know I'd like to have the egg Ava showed me too."

John was already pulling his wallet from his front pants pocket.

"I agree."

Eric smiled as he thought about how he'd show it off at home.

"The egg and the meanings behind all the images would make great stories to tell at home."

By the time Ava returned, peer pressure caused Jacob to cave in. We each decided to buy our own egg, the egg that Ava had each of us analyze. Before we could tell Ava our decision, she presented a goose egg, which was at least 50 percent larger than what we had been examining.

The pitch-black mass that she held in her hand snared our curiosity. Red pointed knives, spears, and arrows launched from each end of the egg, heading to the center. It targeted nothing but empty black space. She turned the egg around. At first, I observed only projectiles flying at and by each other, striking nothing. A closer look exposed many small, red drops falling toward the base of the egg, toward a red lava liquid. Tiny ripples arched out from a few drops, which touched its surface. Examining the drops, one discovered their appearance suggested no pattern, no order, unlike the first egg I studied. Some drops fell from the void, while others slipped off the edge of a knife or the point of a spear. The top of the egg showed a small, round, cloudy, confined, yellowy-white substance.

Cataracts covering an eye.

Grayish-white hairlines scribed Ava's identification along the outer edge of the circle. Her name etched twice inside the cloudy circumference again could easily be mistaken as border design.

"What feelings does this generate?"

Ava's voice was low, as if someone nearby might hear us. We stood still around her creation.

"Fear." Jacob whispered.

"Danger."

John's voice was as low as Ava's.

"Disturbing. Not a place I'd ever what to be," I said wondering what terrible period of history Ava was portraying.

"All of those." Eric said, summing our feelings perfectly.

"What period of history does this egg represent?" John asked as he held the egg, searching it for some hint to the answer for his question.

"The only one I don't feel comfortable talking about," Ava said.

That pulled our eyes to this open storyteller.

"The one I lived through."

Silence blanketed the room. Fear of upsetting Ava silenced more questions.

Finally, Jacob returned the egg to Ava and found his voice. "There is no doubt that this has a major impact on us, but—"

I wondered what Jacob meant by "this." Was it the egg or her comment or both? Jacob told us later that he had hesitated to continue with his next remark.

"But who would want to buy such a disturbing visual?"

"Recently, I owned four such eggs, when a city hotel owner convinced me to sell. I let go of only three of them, even though he offered one thousand Euros for each of them." John and I looked at each other, shocked at the price. Ava seemed to sense our astonishment.

"Businessmen like that have money," she explained.

All we could do is nod.

"He bought other eggs, too."

Ava, letting us photograph the egg, eased us out of our stasis.

I pointed to the other paper carton she held.

"What do you have there?"

When we finished taking pictures, Ava placed the black egg in its cardboard container and then opened the second box. She gave it to me. When I removed the white tissue paper, green and blue greeted my eyes. A warm, multishaded green coated the lower half. The paradise-sky-blue brightened the top half. The random images of the flying birds, butterflies, and small, thin, white clouds implied freedom.

My mind drifted back to times when I was lying on the grass after school, looking up at the sky, and seeing the same thing.

That was a time of no worries, no responsibilities, a good time, I recalled.

The lower green portion, composed of thousands of tiny green strokes, suggested an uncut lawn hiding in a sparse clump of trees. Black rakes and ladders circled the center of the egg, dividing the sky from the earth. Then, an abundance of black deer, roosters, wheat, flowers, pussy willows, and apples were everywhere, as if the wind scattered them like the yellow fall leaves outside her home. Such a profusion of nature's bounty meant wealth, I guessed. This nature scene left the impression of peace and contentment.

Stretching from the bottom of the egg to the top, double green lines divided the egg into quarters. I recalled Ava's instructions earlier in the evening: when you begin to design your egg, first divide the egg into sections. Wrapping around and in between those two green bars was a thick red line weaving its way to the top.

"Looking at your divisions and seeing the two bars painted over some of your symbols, I feel like I'm on the outside looking in. Is that what you meant to convey?"

Ava smiled. Without answering, she instructed me to look at the images on the top and bottom of the egg. An oxidized copper coin crowned the top. When I first saw the coin, I dismissed it as unimportant. I thought it had no place. Turning to the bottom of the egg, a red poppy awaited an admirer. It wasn't a symbol. It was a clear picture of a poppy. Scrambling for meaning, I could only think of opium. From the poppy the red line snaked, weaving in among the green strips.

Sale of drugs?

Reading my bewilderment, Ava explained.

"Present prosperity is not guaranteed. Unless we guard against greed and self-indulgence, darkness will imprison us, bar us from the real blessings in life."

I looked again at the egg with Ava's latest information. I still felt like I was looking in through a window, as if I were witnessing a warm family gathering, something to be treasured. Being able to see the threatening bars implied a needed responsibility. When one knows danger lurks, one prepares to meet it. The egg felt like a poetic warning sign.

"From what you've told me about your grandfather and the stories he shared with you, I thought he might find this egg a source of joy and comfort. What do you think?" Ava asked.

I looked at Ava as she made her case. Her sound reasoning could not dispel the reality that the egg would be way too expensive for us to afford.

"I'm afraid there is no way we could pay for such a beautiful piece of work." I handed the egg back to Ava.

"I only asked whether you thought he would like it?" clarified Ava.

"Oh, without a doubt," I replied, certain that a purchase wasn't an option.

"It would be inappropriate for a lady to give a strange man a gift like this. It would be different if we knew each other for some time. Still, I can't help feeling that, in listening to you, your grandfather and I share so much in common, that I know him." After a brief pause she continued. "What I could do is offer this egg at a gift price, say fifty Euros."

Ava smiled like she'd just solved an enormous problem for me, but I said, "Oh no. We couldn't do that. After all the work that you put into this! It wouldn't be fair to you." I could hear John and Jacob whispering behind me. I assumed they were in complete agreement.

Ava said, "I wish you would reconsider. You'd be doing both your grandfather and me a favor. You know the unique presentation is something that he would appreciate. And you would be giving me a chance to tell him that our life and culture are healthy and growing. We aren't stuck in the past."

I was about the say he'd be disappointed in us for taking advantage of her, when John tapped me on the back.

"Could we have a moment?" he asked, looking at Ava.

She agreed. While John, Jacob, and I met to the side, Eric made his purchase from Ava.

"Accept the deal." John whispered his position with conviction.

I had to look twice at him. Jacob nodded. I still hesitated.

"It's too good a deal to pass up," persisted John. "What's the matter? Don't you have enough money?"

"Don't you think we're taking advantage of her?"

"Not in the least. You heard her. *She* wants us to buy the egg. We didn't try to get her to lower her price. It was her idea."

Jacob's sound logic left me no choice. I opened my wallet, not to see if I had the money for the goose egg, but to see if I had enough for both eggs.

"Do you still intend to buy the first egg she showed you?" I asked.

John's affirmative answer once again surprised me. It turned out that together we had enough money to make the purchase of all four eggs.

"I still felt uncomfortable with paying her so little for the goose egg. Without the other guys knowing I hung back and convinced Ava to accept from us an extra fifty Euros. I said I didn't have it with me, but I would find a way to get it to her. Of course she tried to dissuade me, but when she saw I was serious, she suggested sending the money to her through you. She said she knows and trusts you."

I looked at Natasha to see if she looked surprised. She didn't. But she did smile.

"So, now you know what that envelope is about that I gave you earlier." Natasha nodded. She understood the request I made of her.

At that point I had to tell Natasha I was puzzled. "You evidently know Ava. That means you also have to know that Ava is part of the group that holds the aristocracy responsible for the peasants' poverty. She claimed outright that if it weren't for the church, many more people would have starved to death. The priest often provided food hampers for individuals and socials for the community in times of need. How is it that you can be so accepting of Ava?"

I hoped my evident bias wouldn't annoy her.

"Sounds like quite a contribution for the church to have made."

"That's just what some of the ladies said, too. They were very grateful."

"You'd think the church must have been receiving help from someone in the community, someone with sufficient wealth to pull it off."

I began to think Natasha was referring to the maligned nobility.

"Someone who might have been able to provide a lubricant." Natasha paused and then continued. "For instance say, alcohol to enable the male mask to slip and to allow stories of hunger at home to surface."

"But why wild, drunken parties that sucked the men's money from them?"

"Suck the money from the men and recirculate it to their wives? The fact is, men already met at private places, buying home brew, some of it of poor quality. At times, they'd become so sick they couldn't work the fields. That money they paid enriched only a few people. Some nobles stepped in, including my great-grandfather, and provided their drinking and social establishment, a very large place, with better quality drinks, and at a lower price. Bulk buying has tremendous advantages. The aristocrats' servants became their eyes and ears, a means of assistance."

Natasha remained comfortably seated. Her voice was calm, as if she had faced such challenges before.

Grandfather never hinted at such noble benevolence. Nor had any of the sources I'd talked to in the last three days. I felt Natasha's version of a caring aristocracy needed more evidence to be accepted. All I could come up with was a gracious response.

"I had no idea."

Then, before Natasha could respond, I added, "Nor do the people in the community. Why?"

The latter question came out as if I were an accuser. I felt like an unsolicited advocate for the common people. I wished I'd kept my mouth shut.

"I guess it depends upon where you want to store your treasures, on earth or in heaven."

Natasha allowed a few minutes for that message to take root before she caught my curiosity.

Natasha's Research

"I'll bet there are other stories of noble compassion that you're unaware of," she said.

I had an eerie feeling. Could she read my mind? Did she know I needed more information to accept the concept of a benevolent nobility?

"Like what?"

Natasha leaned closer to me, and in a much lower voice, she began. "Tales of deception are usually restricted to a very select audience, usually only family members. So you won't find this story in any published material. And there are only a few very private family records that can verify it."

Once again she sat back, knowing she'd snared my eager attention.

"You know how this region long ago was frequently overrun by invading armies?"

I nodded. I thought of the Mongols, Tartars, Austria, Poland, Russia, and Germany in World War II.

"At one time, certain nobles wanted to limit not only their losses, but those of their communities. I've researched one noble in particular, a Victor Stephan, who, when faced with a perceived invincible enemy, broke ranks with the rest of the defense force. Understandably, he feared being labeled a traitor. He secretly sent his son Nicolai to speak to the leader of the invading army to negotiate terms of surrender.

"The enemy commander, certain of his victory, was unwilling even to consider the idea. However, the son wouldn't give up. He suggested he knew how the commander could extend his territory to areas greater than he originally considered possible. That earned him an audience. Reasoning that by not fighting he'd have more men available to extend his reach across the land failed to move the commander. The commander's position was that taking new land meant acquiring more resources. If he could have more men *and* resources he'd be interested. Put simply, he demanded a tribute.

"By agreeing to a number of conditions, the son cut the commander's tribute demand of a 50 percent payment of personal property to one of 25 percent from all the peasants under the noble's influence. Nicolai had to point out that people expecting death at the hands of a ruthless invader would likely destroy their own property first, as an act of vengeance. Then the commander's potential return would be much less than he expected if he ignored Nicolai's suggestion.

"The son's second condition was that the noble who does the collecting and providing of verifiable records to the commander, presumably his father, would be subject to only a 10 percent tribute of all his property, including the family members' servants. While that condition was acceptable, the commander proclaimed two nonnegotiable conditions: a deception on the part of the collector would mean the collector would forfeit his life, and the noble's tribute would rise to 25 percent. The commander's second condition was that at least one quarter of the fellow nobles had to accept this same arrangement. To accommodate the latter condition, the son requested that the agreement be written down and signed by the commander.

"The agreement saved many lives and much property. Victor exceeded the noble's quota easily. Nicolai, along with his most trusted knight, visited the hardest-working, richest peasants to explain the negotiated deal. After securing the peasants' confidence, Nicolai proposed a risky alternative. Instead of paying the invader's expected 25 percent, a peasant could hide his property (land, stock, produce, tools) in the noble's property list, the one subject to a 10 percent tribute.

"The perception that a peasant's possessions were few appeared credible, because the peasant agreed to be nothing more than the son's personal servant. To enable a peasant's short-term living requirements to be met, Nicolai provided a nominal amount of currency, a good portion of which wealth a peasant could easily hide.

"When the peasant returned the payment, the remaining share of his property would also be returned. The requirement of a similar payment resulted in Nicolai releasing the peasant from the personal-service commitment. The trusted knight agreed to be designated the collector, thus protecting Nicolai's life."

I had to ask: "What if one of the peasants let the secret out?"

Frankly, I thought Nicolai's actions were ill conceived. Increasing the number of his personal servants seemed a trivial gain. Natasha looked pleased that I attempted to deepen my understanding of her narration.

She continued her history lesson.

"To prevent the service agreement from being exposed, the personal servants all swore to seek out and provide suitable punishment to anyone who betrayed this confidence. You can guess what that might have been."

When Natasha stopped for a sip of her wine, I interjected, "I understand that the noble's son took a huge risk going to meet with the invading commander; but why such effort to save a mere 15 percent? Speaking of risk, why did the noble, Victor, bother to send his son? Why not just surrender?"

"There's more than one way to see it. First, figure meeting the noble wasn't as great a risk as you may think, considering the alternative. Past attacks had proved that the noble's last remaining son could easily have lost his life if there was a battle. It wasn't unusual. As for the secret deal, you could say it made pure economic sense. The more he could save for his people and their resources, the better they all would be able to rebuild and pay more taxes later on. However, one could also say the noble and his son were fulfilling a traditional role handed down from previous generations, using their God-given talents to protect their family, their friends, and their neighbors. They were also protecting their name and their family honor.

"As for the peasants, they weren't taking much of a risk, either. Nicolai had already saved their lives and their property from certain ruin. Then, he dared to propose a scheme that could cost him and his father more in tributes, just to help reduce the peasants' loss. The freedom and property, which he already saved, he then asked them to deposit in the safety of his hands. He even made certain they knew it was in his hands just temporarily, so they had only him to trust. Who better could one trust?"

I wondered if Natasha knew she'd supplied me with a missing piece of the puzzle that allowed me to assume that not all the aristocracy was as self-centered as I had heard. I remained concerned that she always seemed to know what was going on and was ready with an answer. That almost omniscient quality demanded respect, and if I were living under her rule, I suspect I would sense a certain amount of fear.

"Don't you think that Nicolai was some kind of special person?" Natasha asked.

Her unexpected evaluation request caught me off guard.

"Different, at least," I replied.

"Well, the commander's daughter thought he was something special."

Natasha paused.

"She married Nicolai!"

Her announcement left me mystified. For some reason, she appeared to be overjoyed by this event.

To me, having read about arranged marriages for political purposes, the marriage seemed unimportant. Yet Natasha waited for a response from me.

"Good move. It sealed the peace," I offered.

"Probably the rationalization she used to convince her father," explained Natasha proudly.

I suspected Natasha possessed some documentation to support the idea of a romantic interest. I couldn't see that kind of story fascinating Grandfather. I switched subjects.

"I take it their trust was well placed. The peasants' property was returned as was arranged?"

"Certainly. As the nominal payments were made, their property was returned. And their personal service agreements were terminated as payments were made for those who chose to do it." Then, with a smile she added, "Would you like to see the redeeming records?"

I was speechless. This was unbelievable.

"You said you like evidence, remember?" she said.

"You have them?"

"Photos of them, on computer."

Natasha, anticipating my next question, stood up and started toward the door.

"Let's go to my office."

Halfway across the room, she glanced back to confirm my interest. A victorious smile beamed back, compelling me to catch up to her. As we entered her office, Natasha closed the door. She acknowledged that since our last meeting a few days ago, she researched several records.

"I think you'll be impressed with what I discovered."

Once again I stood behind her chair, watching her weave her way through a long series of folders on her computer. A file opened up on the screen, and I bent over to take a closer look. Four columns appeared. Natasha explained that not only the dates, but also the names of the people who had agreed to Nicolai's terms were recorded. She pointed to notations for persons who had reclaimed their surrendered freedom and property. The names and dates that appeared held little meaning for me. I did see, as she quickly scrolled through three pages of lists, there were some blanks by some names.

She placed the cursor on one of the blanks.

"Property and freedoms unclaimed," she clarified. "Some peasants ran away before the invading troops arrived, apparently too afraid the agreement wouldn't stand up."

Natasha glanced toward the door of her office as if to confirm no one lurked near the doorway. Then she activated a new file.

"A personal file," she claimed.

I hovered even closer, feeling like we'd entered a restricted area. I didn't want to miss a thing.

"You've probably already concluded that the noble's son to whom I have been referring is a distant member of my own family. I thought before I go any further I ought to confirm that for you."

The new screen displayed a family tree. It was her family's tree line.

I saw Natasha's name highlighted in bold blue. She has no brothers or sisters. Then, like a blue stream through her family tree, a bloodline worked its way back into history. She stopped scrolling down. In blue, I saw Victor Stephan, the noble who sent his son to negotiate with the commander. Beneath Victor Stephan's name appeared Nicolai and the names of his three brothers. Natalia appeared below Nicolai. Both their names were in blue.

"That's the noble's son, the youngest of his four sons." She explained proudly, pointing to Nicolai. "The others died fighting to defend the region in previous battles. You see, Victor Stephan needed an alternate strategy to meet these invaders, or he'd likely end up with no more sons. That desperate, brave act earned him the respect of his neighboring nobles. None dared to accuse him of treason."

Natasha's voice suggested pride in this pronouncement about her family-honored relative.

She pointed the cursor to a name beside Nicolai.

"Natalia, the commander's daughter."

Her finger pointed out six children in that new family. Natasha's face displayed that fierce pride I'd seen the first day at the registration desk.

"It's surprising what you can find when you go back into your family history, wouldn't you say?"

I agreed.

"Have you ever thought about digging into your family's history?"

Her low voice implied she'd discovered an interesting secret.

I admitted the closest I came to that was listening to Grandfather's stories about times when he and his brothers were kids, and hearing stories he said his grandfather told.

She turned in her chair and looked up at me.

"Maybe I can do you and your grandfather a favor."

The statement hung there as she turned from me back to her computer screen.

I wondered what she meant.

She glanced back to see if I was watching her. Natasha's bright victory smile lit up her face again.

"Let me show you what I found in *your* family tree."

She continued to beam as she read the shock on my face, and then she returned to her computer and called up a new document. As the file appeared on the screen, she slipped out of her chair.

"Sit down and take a look," directed Natasha. "Since this is your family tree I've translated everything into English."

I accepted.

A boldfaced **"Michael"** centered my focus. My brothers' names next to mine weren't boldfaced. I saw my parents' names in bold and so was my grandfather's.

None in blue like hers, I thought critically.

I double-checked the names of the brothers and sisters of my parents and grandfather. Noted under my grandfather's name was the changed name, too. From what I could tell, everything was correct. Unfamiliar boldfaced information followed. Natasha's head neared mine as I stopped skimming over the names.

"Don't stop there," she whispered. "I want you to see how much work I did for you."

I scrolled on, following the bold trail like tracks in the snow leading to the wounded prey. Once again I breathed in the faint scent of her perfume.

We reached the end of the boldfaced trail. I turned in the chair and looked up at her.

"See, at the last name."

I did as she instructed.

"Remember it."

It was Victor Benneshuck. With each arm around me, she tapped a couple of keys, and the Personal Servants Records appeared. Her index finger flew down the computer screen to rest on Victor Benneshuck. Her hand disappeared. She even stepped back as if she expected me to jump out of the chair.

Instead, I sat fastened to the chair, digesting the information. I scanned across the line of my, oh-so-great-great-grandfather. A blank line under Servant clung to his name. The implication prevented me from moving. He'd paid the money back for his property, but not for the release of personal service. Finally, I turned in the swivel chair and looked up at her, conscious that I was occupying her chair.

"Is this for real? I mean is this an actual record of what took place?"

She reached past me and clicked on a couple of keys calling up an ancient document. It was a photo of someone's old, wrinkled "Termination of Personal Service" document.

I recalled seeing something like that at the memory-makers' place. It was framed and behind a plate of glass. It hung on the wall. An elderly gentleman was telling John about it, but I hadn't paid much attention because I came in midway through the story.

Natasha had left room for me to stand up, yet she wore a puzzling smile. It changed from a victory—I got you—to a smile of amusement. I sat speechless, trying to figure out what to do next. To my relief, she broke the silence.

"Historically speaking, your great-great-grandfather's heirs still have an honorable service obligation to my family, but you don't have to worry; there is no legal obligation here. I thought you might want to make an adjustment in our records. I took the liberty of printing this document for you."

She reached into her side drawer and pulled out a paper. An embossed seal at the bottom of the page, to the right of where a signature would be written, made it appear official.

In large, bold, italic script it read:

TERMINATION
OF
PERSONAL SERVICE
OF
MIKE BENNEK (BENNESHUCK)
________ ________________
(DATE) (SIGNATURE)

Natasha took her pen from the desk and dated and signed it. Then she made a brief date entry in the computer.

I felt like a tourist being reeled in by a street vendor. This had the markings of an expensive proposition. I expected the cost to be high. The idea of Natasha standing over me as we entered a round of negotiations felt disadvantageous. I stood up. Being about three inches taller than her, even though she had heels on, made me feel more comfortable asking, "And just what will this cost me?"

Her smile proclaimed she was still in command of this situation and loving it.

"Well, if I remember correctly, you once said you have interesting ways of expressing your appreciation."

To further clarify the situation, she reached up and gave her ponytail a couple of flicks.

"You see, knowledge can make the future brighter," she said.

In an instant, I read the stolen kiss. I grinned. I know thinking she wanted a kiss from me felt a little egotistical, like I was projecting my wish on her. But it was an exciting prospect. In reality, she could have been after money. If it was money, there was a problem. How much? For what? For the last kiss? For the family tree research work? For the just signed document? I chose to read the smile on her face as an invitation for playfulness.

Not wanting to lose out on this golden opportunity, I quickly reached to my back pocket for my wallet. Because I figured I learned so much that I could be thankful for, I doubled the last day's monetary contribution. Without looking up, I returned the wallet, and using the two Euros bills, I created a tight roll. As I expected, she watched me. I'd even guess she enjoyed my repeat performance.

Since she already knew my act, I expected a stop signal after the money slipped into her hair. There was none. She welcomed my kiss. Her arms wrapped around me. We drew each other closer and held on. I enjoyed the feel of every part of her warm body pressed against mine, until I became conscious of her hand slipping into my wallet pocket. I pretended not to notice. In a few moments, I knew she wasn't feeling for my wallet. Following her lead, my hand, too, slipped down to her skirt and started sliding it around, exploring. That development was all too short. Our lips parted, and she bent back. I felt her hands on my chest. My hope that she was looking for my shirt buttons was wrong. Her quick response brought about a premature end to my pleasure.

As we separated, still smiling she pondered out loud, "Maybe I should have kept you as my servant."

Not willing to give her aristocratic position a hope that she would have command over me, I countered: "On the other hand, we may do even better as equal partners."

"Indeed."

She agreed too easily. Her confident response disturbed me. She still knew something I didn't, like I was being teased. First, I had enjoyed a delightful taste, and then it was snatched away. It felt like I just savored a glass of wine and then found out the price for the rest of the bottle was way out of reach.

Handing me my certificate, she announced, "You're free and equal. Go forth and enjoy." I felt like my promotion to equality broke our amorous connection.

Our magic evaporated. She walked to the door of her office and recited my remaining itinerary. I confirmed her recollection as she opened the door. She wished me a safe journey to Kiev and then home.

"If you ever want any help researching your family's history or developing that family tree, feel free to call on me."

I thanked her. After we stepped out of her office, she spoke again, stirring my curiosity.

"Until we meet again."

While that's just another way of saying good-bye, the confident way she said it made me think once again she knew something I didn't. That was her way: knowledge leads to a brighter future. I wanted to question her on what she knew, but I didn't. I dismissed the notion, suspecting that if she knew anything, she wouldn't reveal it until doing so was in her best interest.

I chuckled as I thought of relating this story to Grandfather.

"Grandfather," I imagined beginning my story. "I secured our freedom from personal service to the Ukrainian nobility."

Then I'd show him Natasha's certificate and narrate Natasha's history lesson. Since he was a bit of a history buff, I knew he'd enjoy the story.

Kiev

With no expectation of seeing or hearing from Natasha again, my group and I caught a train to Kiev. We met Josyp Dobrunik, Eric's pen pal, at the Hotel Lybid. He apologized for not meeting us at the train station, but more than made up for it by promising to be our chauffer and tour guide for the next two days. I was surprised to see that he was almost my age. I'd always suspected that he and Eric were about the same age.

Together, he and Eric mapped out our itinerary for Kiev. It began with a two-hour dinner at the Pervack Restaurant, where we became more personally acquainted. Then he took us to St. Sophia Monastery and Cathedral, where he impressed us with his historical knowledge.

Listening to Josyp, one must conclude that this is an important pillar of Ukrainian culture. St. Sophia, the oldest standing stone church, was named after the Greek goddess of wisdom. Prince Yaraslav the Wise built the church to celebrate his father's (Prince Volodomyr's) conversion to Christianity in 988. According to legend, Volodomyr, wanting an advanced religion for his empire, considered three religions.

He rejected Islam because of its restriction on alcohol, and he rejected Judaism because of all its rules. By choosing Christianity, he placed his country in the European sphere instead of the Asian sphere. By choosing to link with Byzantium-Greece instead of Rome, he drew them into Orthodoxy, distinguishing them from the Catholic Poles. That foundational start resulted in over 80 percent of Ukrainians today being Orthodox, even though Catholic Poland ruled for 324 years over Western Ukraine.

Josyp then brought us to the monument of Hetman Bohdan Khmelnisky, the leader of the first Ukrainian War of Independence, the 1654 leader of the kozaks who fought against the Poles. His monument has him as large as his horse and pointing to Russia. To defeat his enemy he aligned himself with Russia as an equal partner. Then, for the next 337 years, Russia repressed the Ukrainian language, culture, and nationalism. We saw the Golden Gate, first constructed between 1017 and 1024, the Holodomyr Memorial, the University of Kiev, and the Shevchenko monument across from the university.

I think I might enjoy reading Taras Shevchenko's work. Besides writing of the beauty of Ukraine's landscape, he boldly challenged the country's Russian and Polish oppressors. He even challenged his own people for putting up with the foreign rulers. What courage! He sounds like Jacob, challenging authority and the way things have always been done. That explains why Jacob refused to work in my father's company. And yet, because we do things as a team, consulting with each other frequently, we easily get along.

The next morning Josyp took us to Pecharaska Lavra, a UNESCO Heritage Site. In 1240, Tartars and Mongols looted and destroyed this Orthodox monastery, which was founded in 1051 by monks. Purchasing a beeswax candle for light, we descended into the underground caves. Mummified monks lined the sides of the tunnels. Tiny rooms with bars over the windows housed monks hidden from the world. We demonstrated reverence by whispering only. There seemed to be a relaxing of the restriction that women cover their heads.

After dinner, we visited the Chornobyl Museum. A factual presentation highlighted the events and the consequences of the explosion. A video showed how and where the wind currents carried the contamination.

Josyp said after that experience we needed something to brighten our spirits. St. Andrews Descent was his solution. This cobblestoned promenade featured shops, kiosks, cafes, and souvenirs. Beautiful paintings and woodwork lined both sides of the street. Three hours seemed to evaporate as we wandered along the two long blocks of works of art. None of us left the area with empty hands. Back at the hotel we treated Josyp to supper and drinks. In the short space of two days he made five new friends.

* * *

The following morning we all boarded the train back to Lviv. Before Jacob arrived, Melissa occupied the seat beside me. Once the train left Kiev, I learned Melissa was very interested in the information I picked up from Ava. She'd heard bits of information from John and Jacob, but she wanted my version. She wanted to know what I thought about Ava and her work, and how I planned to share what I learned with Grandfather. Melissa asked if I was bringing Ava's eggs in my carry-on luggage when we flew home. My affirmative answer brought forth a request to show and tell her about them. I promised to show them to her when we returned to Lviv.

"I hear you have a family tree."

I looked at Melissa, surprised she knew about it.

"Jacob told me," she explained.

"Natasha showed it to me, but I didn't get a copy of it."

Melissa looked disappointed. For a while she didn't say anything. "Jacob said you're thinking about learning Ukrainian."

I told her I was considering taking Ukrainian instruction classes when I returned. She offered to help me. I hadn't even hoped for such support, considering we had spent so little time together in the last year. I began to hope that we might have a future together.

The next day, dinner plans with Uncle Jim and Aunt Susan brought us again to the Nobilis Hotel counter. The same clerk who directed me to Natasha waved a hand, acknowledging our presence. While he finished dealing with another hotel guest, I investigated a bowl of Easter eggs at the far end of the counter. They weren't Ava's.

I thought I'd try to interpret the meaning coded on the eggs. Deep-green geometrical designs painted on the dark, navy background left me with a sense of struggle and hardship, perhaps in the past. Bright flowers and birds meant wishes of good will and fulfillment. Compared to Ava's eggs, the message was simple. I suspected I missed something.

"You're back," greeted the desk clerk. "I trust your research went well."

I nodded.

"Good. Mr. Foresschuck is expecting you.

Suspecting he confused us with another party, I corrected him. "We came to eat dinner with Mr. Jim Chapko."

"And so you shall," replied the desk clerk, confident in his duty. They're both enjoying cocktails in Mr. Foresschuck's suite off the dining area. Just follow me."

I wondered if Mr. Foresschuck knew that Uncle Jim invited all six of us for dinner. Would our numbers make him think he was being taken advantage of? Thinking that Mr. Foresschuck was a regular businessman, I left my group behind to ask the clerk if he knew Mr. Foresschuck.

"But of course. He's one of the owners of the hotel."

My worry disappeared as I echoed Ava's thought: "Businessmen like that have money." I can't think of why I would have forgotten that Mr. Foresschuck was rich. He was an important supporter of the Opera House. I felt stupid. That slipup foreshadowed another moment when I'd make evident my ignorance.

Upon entering the dining room, we recognized Uncle Jim and Aunt Susan sipping their wine. Mr. Foresschuck and his wife, Catherine, gave us a very warm welcome. Mr. Foresschuck began by insisting we call him Will, short for William. After summarizing what he knew about Grandfather's mission for us, he inquired how our research went. I began explaining to him how lucky I was to find a lady by the name of Natasha who greatly aided us.

"Aaahhh, yes. My daughter commented on how energetically you were engaged in your research. You impressed her, and that's not easy to do."

Daughter!

I hadn't made the connection. I recalled glossing over the surnames on the family tree that Natasha showed me. I wondered if he'd detected my ignorance. No sign was evident.

Too gracious to let on, I concluded. Sensing the room temperature had risen a good ten degrees, I considered slipping my sweater off. The sport jackets still worn by Uncle Jim and William Foresschuck forced reconsideration.

"As a matter of fact, Natasha sent me an e-mail, something about forgetting to give you a file."

He moved to a tall side table and accessed his mail account on a computer.

"Here it is," he announced. "Take a look."

It read, "Dad, please bring this file to Mike's attention when he comes over. I think he may want to forward it home. Thanks."

There's another example of Natasha knowing something I didn't. Talk about having the impression of ignorance reinforced! I opened the file. It was my family tree, which she had shown me earlier! I knew Grandfather would love to see it, and I would love to develop it like Natasha had, with footnotes to access primary source documents. I e-mailed the file home and thanked Mr. Foresschuck.

Then we rejoined Melissa, Stephanie, and Mrs. Foresschuck. Melissa had just finished listing the tourist sites we had visited while we were in Kiev.

"I take it your visit to Kiev was well worth it then?" asked Mrs. Foresschuck.

"The sites were very interesting, and Eric's friend, Josyp, was an excellent host. From the historical knowledge he shared with us, I think he'd make an excellent tour guide. He had recommended the Hotel Lybid, took us to the Pervack Restaurant, and concluded our touring by going to the St. Andrew Descent. The creative displays were a treat in themselves."

"So I take it you'd return to Kiev?" Mrs. Foresschuck nodded as Uncle Jim and Aunt Susan joined us.

"To the Ukraine, yes. But not to Kiev."

"Oh! Why not?" Melissa caught Mr. Foresschuck's attention.

"To tell you the truth, I thought some of the people were unfriendly."

"What do you mean?" inquired Mrs. Foresschuck.

"Well." Melissa collected her thoughts for a moment. "You know, I'd asked the Hotel Lybid desk clerk if she knew where the closest place was so I could change some of my American dollars for hryvnia. I asked her in Ukrainian, thinking she'd be impressed a Canadian knew this country's language. You know, she answered me in Russian. I had to ask her in English to repeat her answer so I could understand it. I thought that was very rude of her."

Mrs. Foresschuck opened her mouth to respond, but before she could say anything, Melissa had begun to describe another irritating scenario.

"Then, when we were in the restaurant I asked our server the way to the women's washroom, again in Ukrainian. The lady responded in Russian. I'd have had to guess where to go if she hadn't also pointed to the washroom sign."

I remember Melissa remained upset for the rest of the meal. At the end she demanded no tip be left. Not even Josyp questioned her order.

Without a moment's hesitation, Mr. Foresschuck reflected Melissa's frustration. "Isn't that just like a Russian? It's like they've never given up trying to erase our language, our culture."

"Now, Will!" Mr. Foresschuck's wife's pleading tone had no effect.

"We've finally got our freedom, our independence, and now they are trying even harder to erase our language."

Mr. Foresschuck had taken a breath to continue when he felt Catherine's hand squeeze his arm. In a low voice, Mrs. Foresschuck said, "Will, this isn't the time or place." Her eyes locked into his until he nodded.

"You're right, dear." He lowered his head, acknowledging the wisdom of her instruction.

"You know, Will, we have a similar problem in Canada. We have a province that has only French as its official language." Too late, Uncle Jim caught Mrs. Foresschuck's disapproving eye.

Turning to face Uncle Jim, Mr. Foresschuck picked up from where he left off. "Yes, but your French don't have a history of trying to suppress your language. I'll tell you, if this continues our country will end up being divided or . . ."

"Will!" His wife's stern note prompted an immediate nod. Mr. Foresschuck put his hand on Uncle Jim's forearm and began leading him away from his wife. I caught Aunt Susan smiling. Like me, she suspected the conversation would continue away from Mrs. Foresschuck's ears.

"If language is a problem, how do you work with the government in Kiev? It must be difficult for you." Uncle Jim followed his host.

"You're right; if I had to, it would be frustrating. But I have a friend in Kiev who acts as my agent. He's fluent in both languages."

"Will." Mrs. Foresschuck's call stopped him. When he turned to face his wife, she continued. "Didn't you find a book that you wanted to give to Mike?" She paused, waiting for her husband to recall what she was referring to. "A Ukrainian history book."

"Oh yes—by Magocsi." He flashed a thank-you smile to his wife. Then he looked at Mike. "Do you like to read? The book is in English, and it deals with the origin of the Ukraine to the time of Brezhnev. I found it when I was browsing in the bookstore a few weeks ago. I thought you or your brothers might be interested in it."

"Sounds great!" I thought that was just what I needed to get a background on Ukraine. I suspected Grandfather would start reading it before I got to it. Mr. Foresschuck went to find the book. By the time he came back and gave it to me, the conversation on language had disappeared.

* * *

Ukraine Trip—More Than A Memory

When you have a holiday like the one I just experienced, one with one surprise after another, you should expect that it would haunt you for some time. Sharing the holiday highlights and talking about our souvenirs entertained Grandfather many times. He did take the *History of Ukraine* book that Mr. Foresschuck gave me. I don't know if he finished reading it, though. At home, he kept the egg we brought him on the night table near the alarm clock. He tried to take it into the hospital when he became ill, but Aunt Susan vetoed it. If Aunt Susan hadn't warned me that Grandfather would try to bribe me to smuggle it in, I would have. He settled for me bringing it when I came to see him at the hospital. During those visits, he told me how much he loved hearing me repeat the holiday stories. He was amazed at the interest I showed in our history.

One of his favorite stories was the one about the noble and his son, and the certificate that Natasha signed. He even wanted me to treat it as if it were a government document. He said it should be stored in the safe deposit box in the bank. Grandfather confessed it took him back to times when his grandfather shared stories like that. The stories of hard work and family sticking together comforted him.

I remember telling him shortly after we returned about the family tree that Natasha prepared. It surprised and impressed him, too. The name change filled in some blanks for him. I was surprised that he wasn't shocked by seeing the family tree, as I had been. I asked why?

"Natasha and I talked on the phone. She told me about the tree," he said.

I couldn't believe what I just heard.

"When?" I demanded.

His reply was a simple matter-of-fact response.

"When you were on your holidays. She's very resourceful," he declared with a smile.

I was confused.

"What did she want?"

"Just to talk." Grandfather, seeing I wasn't satisfied, added a little more. "About my past mostly. What I remembered. I confirmed the other members of my family. She even wanted to know about you."

Grandfather sat grinning, as if he were withholding something. I had to pry his secret out of him.

"What?" my faced stopped less than a foot from his. "Tell me." I insisted.

Still grinning he asked, "Did you enjoy the borscht Natasha prepared for you?" Reading the response from my face he added, "She asked to talk to Gram for her recipe."

I tried to convince myself Natasha phoning was just another research technique, a verifying action, but at the same time, her action bothered me. I had lost my privacy. I didn't know how, but I knew I should feel vulnerable.

Grandfather continued. "I told her how proud I was of you. She sounded very impressed with you, too."

I entertained the thought that I should be flattered that she showed such an interest in me.

I informed Grandfather I'd enrolled in a course to learn Ukrainian, one of the results of the trip. He displayed a smile that reminded me of Natasha when she heard I came to research my roots.

I'll always remember his words: "it's more than I dared hope for."

I felt like I just gave him a birthday present, even though it wasn't his birthday.

For a month after we returned from Europe, thoughts of Natasha left me feeling ill at ease. When Jacob and I went for our weekend golf session, I talked to him about my troubling thoughts regarding Natasha. He showed the same surprise I did when he heard Natasha phoned Grandfather. He listened without comment as I related my admiration for her ability to be on top of everything, and my concern over the power she exercised because of knowing ahead of time of the forces shaping my future.

One Saturday, after our game, he spoke in a serious tone I don't often hear from him.

"What's with you? At first I thought your encounter with Natasha worked in your favor. You chose to study Ukrainian. Melissa quit sitting on the fence about her feelings for you. But now I'm beginning to worry about you. You talk about this Natasha as if she is the most amazing person you ever met. You're mesmerized by the interest and energy she devotes to her cultural heritage. You seem to believe she has some ability to predict the future and maybe control some outcomes. It sounds like you see her as some kind of a goddess! What did she do? Cast a spell over you?"

The accusation made me feel stupid, like a kid trying to live a fantasy. I sat in silence.

"Get over it. She's in Europe. You're here. That's the end of it. You'll never see her again. Be glad you have a wonderful girl like Melissa."

It felt like he was the older, wiser brother talking to the younger brother.

"I guess you're right."

I thought about the reality he described. I think I just needed to hear it from someone else. After that talk, I had no trouble sharing highlights of our European research holiday. My mixed feelings evaporated—at least until Uncle Jim talked to me two days ago.

He invited me to his office at the end of the workday, saying he had something important to discuss with me. In response to my "What's up?" he began with "Do you remember when we all went to Europe?"

"That's stepping back in time," I commented, surprised at his topic. Our trip took place five years ago.

He agreed.

"Your life has seen many changes since then hasn't it? You and Melissa married the year after the European holiday. A year after your marriage, you had your first son. A little more than another year later, you had your second son. Then your grandfather died. And now I hear Melissa is pregnant again."

I nodded, not surprised. Uncle Jim usually had his pulse on what was happening in the family.

"Do you think you're ready for another potentially life-changing challenge?"

That enquiry made me straighten up in my chair. I knew this meeting wasn't just a social get-together, but I didn't expect it to be "life changing."

"Like what?"

"Well, I want you to know the invitation I'm about to extend to you wasn't my idea. But once I heard it, I thought it had great potential. First, I want to confirm that everything is completed regarding Grandfather's estate."

I nodded.

"Remember I told you that I met with William Foresschuck about a business venture?"

I nodded again.

"It was to set up a meat processing plant in his country. Everything in our research points to this being an excellent profit maker. I found some investors and dug up contacts for several export markets. Besides investing in the business, he worked through his country's red tape and confirmed suppliers of meat. That took a lot longer than we figured, but he has now cleared all the hurdles."

I congratulated Uncle Jim on his efforts.

He continued. "Last month, I ran into a problem at my end. A situation changed in the life of one of my investors. He dropped out, leaving me short some capital." I could see a request coming for me to use some of the money Grandfather left me in his will. "When I shared my concern in a conference call with Will and his daughter, Natasha suggested I invite you to be an investor. I said I'd think about it."

Jim is my uncle. He needed help. I was all set to ask, "How much?" Then, I heard "Natasha" and bells started ringing in my head. "Until we meet again." That confident phrase that sounded like she knew we would meet again. And her "indeed," and her smile when I said we might make better partners made me wonder what she knew. For an instant I had sensed that we would be partners someday.

Did she find out from Grandfather that he intended to leave a sizeable fortune to his grandchildren? If that were the case, she could have easily used the computer to estimate his fortune. Would she do that? It was her method of operating. *Knowledge makes for an easier, brighter future.* Was the playful move the last time I was in her office an attempt to create a hunger for me to return when she needed money?

". . . your brothers to join us if you like?"

I was suddenly aware that I'd tuned Uncle Jim out.

"Pardon me. I was momentarily distracted."

"I said I don't need an answer from you right away. I know you probably want some time to think about this. It's no small venture. I started with you because of Natasha's suggestion, but I could ask your brothers to join us if you like.?"

I knew I'd want some time to work this out. "How much?"

"One million dollars."

A million! That's exactly what Grandfather had left each of us. Actually, as the oldest son, he'd left me with an extra half million. The instructions in his letter to me were to first use the extra money to help out anyone in the family who was in need, and then build the family's understanding of our heritage. In the letter that came with the will, he declared he had complete faith in me to find a way to preserve and develop our family and cultural heritage. I think he came to understand that I value our culture when I told him I volunteered an extra fifty Euros to Ava for his Easter egg. Right then and there, he stated he was proud of me.

Uncle Jim was right. This potentially life-changing request needed time. I definitely wanted to sort things out.

"Let's just keep this between the two of us for now," I said, and explained I didn't want Melissa or Jacob to start worrying, and that I wanted to think about it first.

He agreed.

* * *

Before I left Uncle Jim's office, I phoned Melissa to let her know I was ordering Chinese food for my supper at the office because I had a problem to work out. I knew she'd think I had some concerns about the shipping schedules or maintenance work on the trucks. There were times I had found problems in what was submitted to me and had to rework the plans. I didn't want Melissa seeing me puzzling over a personal dilemma. It could lead to questions that might get back to Uncle Jim. As I headed to the office, I picked up my usual order from the Chinese restaurant a block away from work.

I sat in my office eating, knowing that money wasn't what worried me about Jim's invitation. I had made no decisions yet about what I was going to do with the money I inherited from Grandfather. If I were to invest in Jim's project, it would have to be for the full million by myself. Asking my brothers to join in might be misunderstood as my wanting to limit possible losses. The perceived impression would cast a shadow on Uncle Jim's investment project. Besides, if we invested as brothers, I would most likely be the family's spokesperson in working with the Foresschucks, meaning I would most likely be working with Natasha. That was my problem. How did I feel about working with her?

Something subtle about her rubbed me the wrong way. While we were in Europe, I hadn't been able to put my finger on it. Since I didn't expect to meet her again, I dismissed my vague concerns. But now I knew I needed to get a handle on it before becoming involved with her again. I suspected I'd have to know everything about how she operated. I would have to study her past, as she no doubt had studied mine. I couldn't leave any dark corners about her so she could surprise me again.

I concluded the best way to prepare myself would be to get all the facts from the holiday down in writing, so I could analyze them clearly. That's when I decided to follow Jacob's suggestion to write the story of our encounter five years ago. I reviewed all the pictures I had downloaded on the computer when I returned from the trip. I wished I had a journal, too. I began the story. That decision glued me to the computer until after midnight. Fortunately, the next day Melissa was so preoccupied with the children she forgot to ask me about the previous night's problem.

The following evening, I remained at work to reread and carefully analyze what I had written. My first impression was that seeing Natasha again would be exciting. Natasha really knew her roots. It increased her pride, giving her something special to live up to. I'm not sure why, but I liked that. And she always had new information for me, causing me to have to rethink my initial impressions. It meant I would have an excellent tutor to guide and rekindle my family tree research.

It was embarrassing to admit: since Grandfather died, I'd done very little to increase my knowledge of our cultural heritage. I hadn't even begun reading the history book I received from Mr. Foresschuck after Grandfather gave it back to me. I let family life and work drown out my initial desire to investigate my family's past accomplishments. It was almost as if my research mission deteriorated into just talking to please Grandfather. That's not what he wanted. But with Natasha, I'd be back on track and energized. That alone would be enough to cause me to jump at this investment opportunity.

Also, Natasha's playful, daring spirit was enticing. She was like a chess opponent who was always planning one or more moves ahead of me. It would be great to have a chance to reverse those tables, to prove to her that a boy of common background is every bit as prepared to meet future challenges as someone with aristocratic blood. In fact, I already did that in Dad's transportation firm. I anticipated and investigated all future possibilities and their consequences before settling on decisions. Dad trusted me completely. That's just what Natasha does.

That's it! I concluded. *I do just what she does. I'm every bit as good as Natasha.*

I knew what bothered me about her: a hint of arrogance, an "I'm-better-than-you-are" attitude. It wasn't what she said directly, but was implied in her words. I was aware of always being directed by her, being told what, when, and how to do it. There was no asking or suggesting. It was like I was one of her servants or employees.

Despite these difficulties, Natasha was so helpful—not only to me, but also to the old ladies in the coffee shop and the elderly memory-makers in the parish church. Natasha could've given me all the information I was looking for. Instead, she gave them a chance to practice their English and to proclaim the triumphs in the lives of their families.

She also demonstrated her kindness in her story about the efforts of the noble's son, Nicolai—when he tried to reduce the tribute the peasants would have to pay. That was it, the thing that bothered me most. All her stories illustrated how the aristocrats had the interests of their neighbors and their heritage at heart. While I don't doubt the truth of the stories, I was led to infer from her way of telling of them that no one else had that quality.

I wonder if Natasha's conversation with Grandfather opened her eyes to the possibility that ordinary people like my grandfather or our family also highly value our cultural background. Could that be the reason why Grandfather changed his will to provide me with the extra half million dollars, to pick up where he left off in leading our family into a greater awareness of our roots? He probably suspected Natasha would spur my efforts.

* * *

I knew I had to get a hold of Grandfather's will again. My reaction upon hearing about the distribution of money to the family when the will was read, and when I read Grandfather's personal letter to me about the extra half million, now seems to have been immature. I vaguely remembered Grandfather leaving donations to various Ukrainian organizations. He must have been supporting their development in other ways, too.

Grandfather's philanthropy is another area of research I should be looking into. How much did he give away, to whom, and how often? How was he involved? What were the organizations he gave to doing? Grandfather never talked much about what he did. He was far too modest. The exciting thought of pursuing those questions made me think of Natasha again, of the work she'd done researching her past, and the pride that it created in her. I too could strive for such goals, starting with Grandfather's life. With Natasha's help I could go beyond his life. That would also show her that regular people can be thrilled with their families' past accomplishments. More importantly, Grandfather would rest in peace now, seeing I was honoring his wishes.

I can now see Grandfather, the successful businessman, planting the seed of love for our heritage in me by sending me to Europe. He became the seed's sunshine when I returned. Natasha was the rain that encouraged the growth while I was in Europe, and now that Grandfather was gone, she will be both the sun and the rain.

This investment proposal is just what I need. I have to tell Uncle Jim I will be in on it. It is safe to say it provides an excellent opportunity for me to grow financially and culturally. I can even say I felt like I am ready to meet the challenge of working with Natasha in the spirit Grandfather would have had me do it.

With my decision finally made, I allow myself the luxury of remembering some little details about Grandfather's last years. Certain images and phrases keep reappearing to me. Write this down!

Words drop onto a piece of scrap paper. Playing with them results in a poetic tribute.

Grandfather's Last Years

The last grains of sand
weighed heavily on
thin, white-haired Grandfather.

Too late
for Grandfather's drained body
to convert his son, lover of mammon;
too late
to carry the ancestral torch
himself.

Little time left
to mine past taxing trials—
pillars for an altering future.

A cash gift fertilizes
rooting around in the old country,
soaking in their sun,
ripening into celebration fruits,
to honor
his treasured heritage and
sprouting Ukrainians' creations.

Growing grandchildren graft
to a generation steeped in tradition.

A Reader's Questions for Contemplation

1.At the beginning of Mike's story, what do you think Mike's concept was of the Ukrainian heritage? How had that concept changed by the end of the story?

2. Describe what you think was Grandfather's idea of the Ukrainian culture. In what way would Grandfather be pleased about Mike's increased understanding of the Ukrainian heritage? In what way would he have been disappointed in Mike's knowledge about his roots?

3. What are the important attributes or strengths of your family's heritage? Evaluate how well that heritage has been passed on from one generation to the next.

4. Family was an important value for Grandfather. What evidence do you find in the story to show that that value was shared by others in Grandfather's family?

5. Melissa's interest in Mike grew. What do you think caused that growth? What evidence from Mike's story supports your position? When do you think that interest started?

6. Were Mr. Foresschuck and Mr. Kupchenko, being good hosts to Mike and his entourage or do you think there were other motives for their gracious actions? If so what were those motives?

7. What are the strongest elements in the dominant North American culture that sap time and energy from following one's own family culture?

8. What are the strongest elements of one's past that enables a people to preserve their heritage?

9. Is there any particular age when one realizes the importance of one's past heritage? If so, what age is that and why?

10. Grandfather instructs Mike that he should be a leader in the company. That means, at times, he should promote his culture's values. Doing this together around Thanksgiving time was the specific issue that Grandfather referred to. Are there any values in your own or another's culture that should have an impact on the dominant culture? If so, what are those values, and why should they have an impact?

11. What response would you expect to come from Shevchenko (1814-59), the Ukraine's outspoken nationalist, with respect to the recent efforts of the Ukrainian government's attempts to recognize Russian as an official language of the Ukraine?

12. As Ukraine is a democracy, and the heart of democracy is finding reasonable compromises, do you think that Shevchenko, Pawelo, or Mr. Foresschuck would be willing to look at how the United States handles the growing importance of Spanish in their society as an acceptable accommodation? Would the Canadian federal government's policy toward French in Canada be an acceptable accommodation for Ukraine?

CPSIA information can be obtained at www.ICGtesting.com
Printed in the USA
LVOW132255121112

307001LV00001B/11/P